G000122801

Wandering Stars

By Rachael Hohf

Copyright © 2021 Rachael Hohf

All rights reserved. The characters and events portrayed in this book are fictitious. Any similarity to real persons, living or dead, is purely coincidental and not intended by the author.

No part of this book may be reproduced, stored in a retrieval system, or transmitted in any form or by any means, electronic, mechanical, photocopying, recording, or otherwise without express written permission of the publisher.

Cover Design by: Rachael Hohf; cover photo © Adobe Photostock

Printed in the United States of America.

CONTENTS

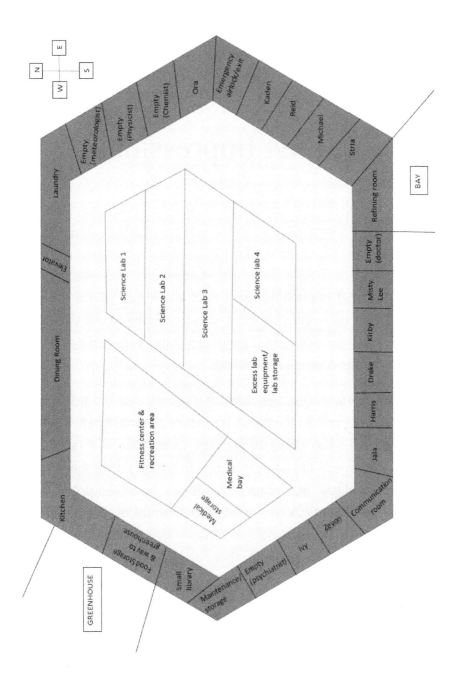

1: First Impressions

D r. Amat opened her dark eyes and forgot where she was for a moment. The slow, steady rocking of the shuttle as it settled down on their landing site reminded her of the ocean's rhythmic waves back home.

Not a day at the beach, she reminded herself, but the first day of her three-year research mission on Saturn's moon, Titan; the only other place in the Universe besides Earth that had lakes and oceans. Not made of water, though—these seas were made from "liquid natural gas" according to her NASA- approved pre-mission trainer. He'd meticulously explained that all of Titan's liquids were a mixture of methane and ethane, and that the lakes were so cold anything that landed in them would instantly freeze solid.

She assumed the oceanographer in their little party would be eager to get started. It was interesting enough that Ora herself wouldn't mind examining the lakes, even though as a paleontologist, she had no idea what she should be looking for.

She allowed herself a few more minutes inside the peaceful sleep chamber to let her mind come back to full consciousness. Gazing lazily through the hazy silicone barrier, she noted that Dr. Kaden Meade was already halfway out of his sleep chamber and talking excitedly, even though she couldn't hear him through the cocoon's silicone sound barrier.

It was a mystery to Ora how his lanky frame had been crammed into the small cryo-cocoon in the first place.

✫✫✫✫✫✫✫✫✫

Kaden stretched himself out for about fifteen minutes and walked the length of the too-small shuttle before he felt some of the cramps start to work themselves out of his long legs.

As smothering as those cocoons were, Kaden felt being wrapped inside asleep was better than being fully awake and roaming the tiny ship for the full seven-year journey. He would've gone crazy walking the small circle that doubled as their command center and sleeping quarters.

The gauzy lid of the remaining cryo-chamber slid silently open as the third occupant of the small craft slowly raised herself into a seated position. Kaden was so excited someone else was awake that he finished an entire speech about the marvels of space travel before she'd even glanced in his direction.

Stria Reese was silently taking in the enormity of it all, her cornflower blue eyes wide with anxiety. She suddenly realized that it was one thing to prepare to go to another world, but it was another thing entirely to actually **be** on another world.

She barely registered the fact that somebody was talking about something at a rapid clip. It didn't seem to matter whether she responded or not, so she didn't. Instead, she allowed her mind to drift far away as Kaden's constant babble ebbed and flowed in the background.

Back on Earth it had been so thrilling to think about being on a world so entirely different from the only one she'd ever known!

She looked out at the alien landscape, a hazy orange jumble of rocks and sky that didn't seem very welcoming. It wasn't quite as exciting now that those alien lakes she'd studied in color-enhanced photographs were lurking only a few miles away, threatening to turn anyone who was clumsy enough to fall in into a rock-hard ice sculpture.

She began to braid her light brown hair in an effort to force down an aggressively rising panic attack brought on by the realization that there was no escape. Whatever happened, she was trapped here for three years until their research mission was complete. Her fingers undid the unruly braid and compulsively started a new one.

Stria thought she remembered something about a shuttle coming next year to take the current group of scientists back to Earth. Maybe she could convince one of them to trade places with her, and let her leave on next year's shuttle instead.

After all, she could manage a year up here, couldn't she? But first she had to make it through today...

What if the special suits we're supposed to wear don't protect us against the subzero temperatures? What if microscopic hydrocarbon particles get inside my suit? How do we know there aren't any alien bacteria on this moon, ready to attack our little army of Earthen invaders? These thoughts raced frantically through Stria's mind.

Her fingers gripped the three strands of hair they were weaving even more tightly. She hadn't spent much time thinking about the fact that she was giving up the clear blue skies of Colorado for the oppressive tangerine smog of Titan. Not when she was on Earth, anyway. Now these unpleasant thoughts came fast and thick.

Nothing green to look at, no birds in the sky—not even insects to buzz past her ears. Only empty, dead lakes and rock-hard ice pebbles covered in orange and black particulates.

Trapped...trapped for three years. No one to help us if something goes wrong! Why did I come?

The sheer desperation in these thoughts surprised her. She'd had little moments of anxiety from time to time on Earth, but nothing like this. The only thing that kept her hanging on, barely, was the braid her hands kept remaking and the fear of looking crazy in front of her colleagues.

She was supposed to be a world-class oceanographer, after all, not some silly scared little girl who thought she'd seen a monster under the bed. Stria was worried her travel companions could see how close she was to blasting through the shuttle door and running off into Titan's opaque orange silence, filling it with her terrified screams.

☆☆☆☆☆☆☆☆☆

"Dr. Reese, so nice to finally meet you! We've heard so much about you this past year from Mission Control and couldn't wait to get you up here. You know what a topic of fascination Kraken Mare and Ligeia Mare have been since we first discovered they contained liquid. We hope that with your expertise, we'll unlock a lot more secrets about these seas!"

Station commander Jala Shan extended a thickly gloved hand in greeting and beamed the most welcoming smile she could manage through the thick silicone visor of her spacesuit. Instead of replying, Dr. Reese simply stared fixedly at the strange flatness of the nearby sea, almost black in the filtered tangerine light.

There should be waves, she thought dimly. *Why aren't there waves?*

In spite of the sense-numbing space suit, Stria could tell there was a breeze blowing because the little particles around her feet danced in slow motion toward some unknown destination—but the liquid was nearly smooth.

Saturn leered mockingly in the smoggy sky above her, rings visible. *I don't belong here; I don't know what I was thinking in coming here,* she thought helplessly.

Commander Shan recognized that glassy-eyed expression—it was something that happened to many of the civilians the first time they arrived. It *was* a lot for newcomers to take in—the air pressure was slightly heavier than Earth's, so it always felt like you were walking around at the bottom of a shallow lake. And certainly, the lack of warmth (it was a chilly 290 degrees below zero year-round) and weak sunlight (lost in the smoggy orangish twilight of Titan's air) took some getting used to.

Visibility was about five miles on a good day; on bad days, it was like being caught in a thick, ochre fog. And when it rained...well, that was something the newcomers would have to experience for themselves.

Unfortunately for Stria, Jala wasn't the only one who'd noticed how tightly wound the scientist was. Dr. Amat felt slightly embarrassed by her colleague's apparent collapse now that they were on Titan.

How did she manage to pass the psych tests to get approved for a long-term assignment? Ora wondered. *The poor child looks like she's going to fall apart, and we haven't even made it through our first day yet! Thankfully, Kaden appears to be taking everything in stride, as he should be. But Stria—how on Earth, er Titan, did she make it past the evaluators?*

Commander Shan also approved of Dr. Meade. He, at least, seemed to have the right spirit about things—he was already looking around at the nearest "rock" formations and gesticulating happily to his companions, looking like a refugee from the Wizard of Oz. *Yes, that's it! Dr. Reese is like Dorothy...not in Kansas anymore and not sure she likes it. And, of course, Kaden is the tall, awkward Scarecrow.*

Commander Shan turned away from the dazed oceanographer with some relief and welcomed this energetic young man. He wasn't frightened of this place at all, and seemed genuinely glad to be on Titan. He kicked the ground a few times in order to watch the dirt move around, then reminded himself that this wasn't really dirt—it was the same material that made up the haze floating all around them.

When the particles got too heavy to stay in the sky, they lazily made their way down to the moon's surface. As such, it, too, had an orange tint to it.

Under that layer of material, he knew, lay ice as hard as solid rock. At least, that's what he was partly here to determine. New discoveries awaited him at every turn! This was the opportunity of a lifetime, and Kaden wasn't about to take it for granted. He was ready to make a name for himself on this far-flung moon in a way he hadn't been able to on Earth.

The Commander, who flattered herself on being able to judge who would be successful on her station, was torn over Dr. Amat. She was an interesting woman—not afraid of being here, but not overly enthusiastic about it, either. At least she shook hands firmly enough and responded more appropriately to the Commander's greeting.

"I'm the paleontologist," Dr. Amat added superfluously, hoping it would prod their host to tell her why NASA felt it was so necessary for her to be here.

"Yes, yes, the oceanographer, the geologist, and the paleontologist. Everyone present and accounted for," Jala said briskly. "Now, if I can tear Dr. Meade away from his studies," Jala added, giving Kaden a gentle nudge, "we'll get you all into the refining room at the Station and will have you settled into your quarters before supper."

Kaden looked abashed and obediently joined the group at the rover. *There will be plenty of time for exploring later,* he reminded himself.

Commander Shan hopped effortlessly into the front seat of the waiting rover. Once she was satisfied that the newcomers were properly situated, and no arms or legs were outside the safe zone, she pressed a bright blue button on the main console. The vehicle's roof quickly folded down around them, protectively encasing the rover's frame in a flexible, shimmering white substance.

"What is this stuff?" Dr. Meade asked wonderingly. "It's like we're on the inside of a balloon!" he said gleefully, looking out at a slightly less-orange landscape.

"This is one of our latest inventions, and we're all quite proud of it here," explained the Commander. "We all felt a bit too exposed to the elements in these rovers before. The bubble around us is made from a substance similar to rubber. We created it from the hydrocarbons on the moon's surface. It keeps the particles of haze—and the rain! —out, without collapsing. And, it's still flexible enough to mold to any shape we put it over. Pretty amazing, right?"

Not waiting for a reply, she turned back to the control panel and pressed a flashing green button with her left hand, while guiding a rollerball forward with her right.

With barely a whisper, the rover merrily bounced them toward the reflective white hexagon they recognized as Titan Station Zero.

"This—is—awesome!" whooped Kaden. *Just like mudding back home in Iowa*, he thought happily. *This place'll be alright.* Titan was living up to all his expectations so far.

Stria, sitting in the back with Dr. Amat, was not enjoying herself nearly as much.

The station, which had been designed to contrast sharply with the surrounding landscape and act as a beacon when the fog got especially heavy, was zooming toward them with surprising speed. The passengers could see an oscillating light sending out white pulses like an old-fashioned lighthouse, piercing the smog for miles.

"How appropriate," said Dr. Amat, speaking quietly to Stria. "The original planners were far-thinking, providing a way home in case any of us should happen to accidentally lose our way."

"I don't know why you're addressing that comment to me," Stria said in a strained voice, fear dilating her pupils.

"I thought you, most of all, might appreciate knowing that there's always a light to guide us home," Ora said in slight annoyance.

"Look, it's no secret that you're struggling. I'm just trying to help you—and give you a little advice. Don't let your fear get the best of you up here. None of us can afford it."

Gazing meaningfully at the younger woman until Stria looked away, Ora wrinkled her brow with concern. *If she isn't fit to be up here, she could do us all harm. I told Mission Control those psych evals weren't foolproof. You can't gauge whether someone's ready for a long-term space mission from a 2-hour interview and a set of electrodes monitoring brainwaves and heartbeats.*

Almost at the base now, they could see a wide bank of windows snaking around the building, lights winking at them here and there through a few of the clear panes. Pointing to a low, frosted structure near the base of the Station, Stria asked, "Is that—a greenhouse?" with her first sign of animation since they'd landed.

"Of course! You don't think we could feed ourselves long-term without one, do you? And, although I consider them a waste of space, we even have a few flowers."

"And...anyone can go into the greenhouse?" Stria asked, flushing at the intense scrutiny she was getting from the Commander. She knew how stupid it must sound to be so excited about a greenhouse you could find anywhere on Earth when she was supposed to be excited about the seas that could only be found here.

Commander Shan eyed her with concern. "Ye-es, certainly, though I doubt you'll have much time for wandering around the kitchen's greenhouse once you settle down to your work," she said in a bright but slightly forced tone. She was worried about this one.

Dr. Reese was likely to be a runner—one of those scientists who couldn't handle the fact that they were on another world. They always seemed to sneak out at night, running away in their suits (if they were still sane enough to grab one) and slowly starving to death out on the frozen moon. Or—if they'd been stupid enough to leave without the protective suit—dying almost immediately from the intense cold and lack of oxygen.

She kind of preferred the ones who ran in their suits—they usually made it far enough away from the station that the other scientists never had to see their dead bodies. Jala shivered slightly.

Disposing of the bodies is the worst part, she thought darkly. And now they might have another one if Stria couldn't figure out a way to get herself calmed down.

Expertly guiding the rover into the large, enclosed parking bay attached at right angles to the hexagonal station, Commander Shan backed into Rover 7's designated area as the heavy bay doors closed slowly behind them.

While the bay was a little lighter than the gloomy twilight outside, the halogen lamps didn't do much to chase away the shadows that gathered in the corners of the building like hungry rats.

Stria was becoming even less comfortable than before, if that was possible. She hurried to catch up to the rest of the group, already at a cluster of buttons and levers on the far side of the hangar doors.

"Now this code," the Commander was saying firmly, "locks the bay doors, and a second code activates the airtight vacuum seal." She quickly entered two short numerical codes into the tiny touchscreen in the wall. "Hold on—several ducts will open at varying heights around the bay, and have been designed to pull as many contaminants outside as possible. They can easily drag a person right through the vents if you're not careful."

The newcomers dutifully reached for the conveniently placed metal rungs near the instrument cluster.

"Once you see the airlock signal turn green, like so," as she pointed to the glowing green rectangle below the illuminated touchscreen, "the ducts have done their job and you can activate the climate system."

She had Dr. Amat pull down firmly on a black lever to the right of the green airlock signal, and the group could hear the welcome whoosh of air flooding into the room.

Dr. Meade could hardly wait to get out of his awkward space suit and explore more of the station, and eagerly began to twist off his helmet.

"Wait!" The Commander shouted. "Not until the airlock button changes to purple—now it's safe to remove your helmets and take your first breath of Titan Station Zero's air."

Placing their helmets in lockers already labeled with their names, the three scientists were also instructed to remove their space suits and the heavy shoes that came with them.

"How do we know we haven't brought any of the moon's particles inside the bay with us?" Dr. Meade asked. "I think I may have gotten a little dust on my clothes from taking off the spacesuit."

Stria breathed a quick sigh of relief—at least she wasn't the only person worried about that. She shot a grateful glance in Kaden's direction.

"That's what the Refining room is for," the Commander replied. "Please hurry—we've only got a few seconds after removing the spacesuits to get decontaminated."

"Or what?" asked Dr. Amat.

Ignoring the question, Commander Shan pressed her palm against a scanner set into the only door leading into the space station. "Welcome, Commander Shan," the scanner greeted mechanically, and she rushed them into the room without speaking.

"Oh, this is not what I thought we'd find at all!" said Stria, giggling a little at the strangeness of everything they'd been through so far.

"No talking once the process begins!" snapped Commander Shan.

Fitting gigantic black visors over their eyes, they were each instructed to step into one of the aquamarine rectangles outlined on the gleaming white floor. Opaque walls rose from the sides of each rectangle, neck-high, partially hiding the others from view. A bright light flashed briefly, disintegrating whatever they'd worn in with them, but leaving their hair and skin unharmed.

The scientists saw the wisdom of keeping their mouths shut as a warm, green liquid oozed slowly down on them from some hidden place overhead, enveloping each of them from head to toe in thick, sticky slime. This, too, was dispelled by the bright light, and they were then lightly dusted in a sparkly silver material that turned from powder to liquid when it was touched. One more flash of light removed all trace of the silver sparkles, and a recess opened in one wall of each rectangle, displaying a new uniform with each scientist's name on it.

Clothed once more, Jala said, "If you could all put on the uniforms provided for you—I think you'll see they all fit perfectly—you'll find a small oval in the recess that will lower your rectangle's walls when pressed. Good, I see everyone is ready to enter the station. Follow me to your individual quarters, then."

"Oh, your uniform is light blue—I thought we'd all have the same color."

"Blue for the ocean, since I'm the oceanographer, I guess? That's a little too on the nose, don't you think? Especially since you're stuck with earthy tan, and you're..."

"The geologist," Dr. Meade chimed in. "Hmm, well, I didn't know fossils were yellow," he winked, taking in Ora's buttery uniform, and appreciating the way it complimented her neat black hair.

"Yellow happens to be my favorite color," said Ora with a slight smile. *The young always want to joke away the unknown. A standard, but tiring, coping mechanism.* She sighed inwardly.

More than ever, she felt her age—not that she was old at 42, but lately she'd found that she had less and less in common with the twentysomethings she was often surrounded by.

Paradoxically, she sometimes caught herself wishing she were a young, carefree woman again, before she'd experienced enough of the world to be weighed down by her choices and still felt hopeful about the future. But now she was living in the future her younger self had daydreamed about in those long-ago days, and it wasn't living up to her youthful expectations.

Instead, she felt disillusioned and a little sad. Not that being on one of NASA's research moons was anything to sneeze at—it was a great honor to be here and very few scientists ever ended up actually being chosen, let alone recruited as she had been.

What's wrong with me? Really, I've lived a very interesting life so far, and accomplished nearly all of the things I wanted to do. And this is one more step on my upward journey.

She tried to focus on the positive aspects of this new step, but couldn't help feeling like something was missing in her life. Hopefully, her time on the station would be fulfilling enough to banish these silly thoughts from her mind. After all, what could she have possibly missed out on?

"We aim to please," assured Commander Shan, choosing to ignore whatever storm was passing through Ora's head, and speaking in her best, "Aren't we all having fun, children?" voice for Stria's benefit.

She'd changed into a form-fitting uniform of jade green that somehow made her seem as unattractive as possible, in spite of hugging her well-formed curves.

"You'll find that each specialty area has a different color uniform. For example, our station engineers both wear gray. Our two chefs wear red uniforms, and my assistant wears jade green, to match my own. I never asked him how he felt about it, but he doesn't seem to mind," she smiled.

Pressing her hand to a nearly hidden wall scanner, she led them into a surprisingly spacious and brightly lit hallway, giving them a second to take in the grandeur of the space station. Just as everyone else did, this group of new arrivals stared in awe at the well-equipped science labs and workout facility dead ahead in the hexagon's center.

She watched as their eyes trailed up the sharply angled walls to the high, curved ceiling thirty feet overhead. There were no skylights...the architects decided it would be too depressing to look up and see a perpetual orangish haze instead of the bright blue sky Earthlings were used to.

So, to lighten things up, the ceiling had been painted robin's egg blue, and at "night," the ceiling darkened to a deep indigo and tiny, recessed lights that were off during the day slowly brightened up the night "sky" of the station. It wasn't quite like stargazing back home, but it had been enough to keep more than one person sane on their long sojourn here.

Commander Shan explained, as proudly as if she'd been one of the architects herself, the many unique features of the station. She loved its hexagonal shape, and described in great detail the ring of rooms around the outside, noting that each room opened onto the free zone in the center.

The free zone was split into the two areas they were staring at now: the combination fitness center and medical area toward the north end of the building, and the four science labs they were currently drooling over. The walls of the labs were a special type of shatter-proof glass, and as such, you could see all the way through to the living quarters along the outer ring of the hexagon.

Stria, who'd been intently watching her companions to keep her own emotions in check, saw Kaden's eyes light up over each new revelation.

"I know there must be a lot of machinery all around us to keep this place running, but I can't hear any of it," said Dr. Amat, impressed by the level of craftsmanship and forethought put into the station.

"Ah yes, all of the exterior walls have been lined with a special sound-proofing material, as well as the interior walls of all the living quarters—and the dining room. It's similar to the silicone-based cocoons you slept in on your way here. We wanted to provide all the comforts of Earth here on Titan, and the steady buzz of machinery would have been quite out of place! Providing a home-away-from-home was also why we searched for five-star chefs to cook all our meals. None of those gritty, dry MREs for this station!

"We even have a crew member whose sole job is to take care of the station's laundry and cleaning needs. She also controls the cleaning drones you see around you, ensuring that everything is sanitized and spotless. In addition, our two first-class engineers make sure that our ventilation and heating systems are in perfect working order, as well as handling any upkeep to the machinery that's housed here. As you can see, we've taken every precaution to ensure the safety and comfort of our crew and guests."

Stria risked taking her eyes off Kaden's awed face for a moment and followed Commander Shan's outstretched hand, pleasantly surprised that the interior of the space station wasn't made from the same gleaming white material used in the Refining Room.

Instead, the walls had been painted a peaceful shade of fern green, with hints of gray mixed in. It almost made her feel like she was in a forest, and with the abundance of large, potted plants placed strategically around the station's outer ring, it almost looked like it, too. She closed her eyes and imagined she could hear the sounds of a tropical rainforest, picturing brightly colored birds peeking through the tall foliage.

Kaden's appreciative "oohs" and "ahhs" pulled her unwillingly back to her current reality. Unable to contain himself any longer, Kaden practically shouted, "This place is amazing!" and almost ran into one of the clear glass walls of the nearest lab in his excitement. Looking at Ora and Stria, he was slightly disappointed not to see his own enthusiasm mirrored in their eyes.

"See, no reason to worry," Ora said quietly to Stria during one of Kaden's rapturous outbursts. "It appears to be quite peaceful here."

Knowing that her new guests would be exhausted after experiencing Titan and the space station for the first time, Commander Shan led them to what would be their quarters for the next three years. They reached Stria's room first, much to her relief. It had all been incredibly overwhelming and she wanted to be alone for a few moments to gather her thoughts.

Saying goodbye to the group, and getting a reminder that meals were served on Earth time, not Titan time, Stria figured that left almost an hour to herself. *Thank goodness.*

Not that the others weren't nice, but Kaden's exuberance over everything they'd seen and done so far was getting on her nerves. And she didn't appreciate Ora patronizing her, trying out soothing tricks she'd picked up in some high-school psychology class.

Stria really wished Ora hadn't come—or that she herself hadn't come. But there was nothing she could do about either of those things now.

Frowning, she sat down dejectedly on the edge of the twin-sized bed and pouted, just like a child away at camp for the first time. *I don't like Ora very much. I wish there were more people here, so I didn't have to see her so often. I'll have to be on my guard all the time around her so I don't have to listen to any more of her 'helpful' platitudes about lighthouses or whatever she thinks will make me feel better.*

She sighed and looked around at the room she was to occupy for the next three years. *At least our rooms are decent,* she thought with grudging appreciation.

There was a large window that she could cover up with thick gray curtains if Titan became too overwhelming. The walls were a pale Earth-sky blue, with a truly breath-taking painting of the Pacific Ocean on one side, and a smaller photo of Titan's Kraken Mare on the other.

Those formations jutting out into the black liquid were quite interesting—that was something she hadn't seen in any of the photos she'd studied on Earth. *I wonder what caused those?* she thought, her analytical side kicking in and pushing her fears aside for the moment.

A comfortable looking armchair sat directly beneath the painting, covered in the same shade of gray as the curtains. Her comforter matched them both but was incredibly velvety and smooth to the touch. *They sure love gray here,* she mused, noting that even the thick-piled carpet was the same color. She slipped off her socks and shoes, and let her bare toes sink into that luscious carpet. *Maybe this won't be so bad,* she thought cautiously, her mind quieted for the first time since they landed.

✯✯✯✯✯✯✯✯✯

Dr. Meade was three doors down from Stria—the station's lead scientist, Dr. Kinney, and Dr. Kinney's assistant had the two rooms in between them. He was quite vocal in exclaiming how incredible his room was, and the Commander and Dr. Amat left him in the doorway praising its virtues.

While set up in the same way Stria's room had been, his walls were light brown, and the curtains, armchair, comforter, and carpet were all a rich shade of burgundy. Kaden's room featured a painting of Mount Vesuvius in mid-eruption on one wall, and his photograph showed one of Titan's cryovolcanoes, spewing water-ice and ammonia over the Titanean landscape.

Like his colleague's room, there was a closet full of his new uniforms, and a dresser he could put his limited personal belongings into once they'd gone through quarantine. If he wanted music, the time (on Earth and Titan), games, or anything else to entertain himself, he simply had to hold a small white disk in his hand, and then reach out for the item he wanted from the 3D menu that appeared in the middle of the room.

Boy, this is the life, he thought. *So much better than my boring old life on Earth. I never could've afforded to stay someplace this nice back home. I wonder if they'll let me stay past my three-year limit?*

He happily played with the entertainment options until the dinner chime sounded.

☆☆☆☆☆☆☆☆☆

"Now Ms. Amat, I think you'll find that your room will be quite satisfactory, and we've made every effort to keep your preferences in mind," beamed Commander Shan, feeling the familiar rush of pride that came with showing her station off to the new arrivals.

Sweeping her hand over a small, illuminated rectangle in the wall, the door whooshed open, revealing a neat room with pale, buttery yellow walls, well-made curtains, a cozy-looking armchair, thick sound-numbing carpet, and a luxurious comforter all done in a pleasing shade of gold.

They really went overboard on the whole yellow thing, Ora thought, slightly amused. *I guess I'd better be careful what I tell them I like.*

Feeling that her job was done for the afternoon, Jala had already turned away in search of her Assistant Commander when Ora latched onto her arm and pulled Shan back around. She wasn't willing to let her leave without asking the one question that had been on Ora's mind since her training sessions back on Earth.

Jala turned startled eyes to the newcomer—she wasn't used to being manhandled this way.

"Look, I need you to be honest with me. Everyone knows there's no life on Titan—at least nothing larger than a microbe, so why go through all the trouble and expense to bring me up here? I couldn't go anywhere on Earth without NASA staff bumping into me somewhere they shouldn't have been and asking me to join the mission. Begging, actually. Do you know what I'm getting paid to be here?"

Commander Shan shrugged her shoulders—what anyone was or wasn't getting paid really didn't matter to her. The scientists were all transients, anyway. Here for a bit and then gone. Jala was already on her third group of scientists with this bunch, and the novelty had worn off. She really didn't care if any more scientists came up here at all. She was sure that she and Harris would've been perfectly capable of handling any experiments NASA needed, and felt that sending up group after group of over-educated, condescending intellectuals was a waste of everyone's time and money.

Seeing Jala's lack of interest deeply irritated Ora. "Why can't you understand how strange this is?" she nearly shouted.

"My specialty is prehistoric life—and everyone knows there were never any dinosaurs here! You already have a world-class microbiologist on staff who's far more qualified to handle any little hints of life that might come up than I would be. It doesn't make any sense for me to be here!" she repeated in exasperation.

"And yet, here you are, whether it makes sense to you or not," replied the Commander stiffly. "I think you'll find that not everything on Titan will 'make sense' to you, so you'll have to figure out some way to cope with your disappointment. By the way, you've only got about thirty minutes to freshen up before dinner."

She released herself from Ora's vice-like grip with a sudden twist and an icy smile and walked off in search of Assistant Commander Adley.

First order of business, thought Ora angrily behind her closed door, *is to knock that smug smile off the Commander's face. How hard would it be to give me a straight answer? Shan probably does a fine job of making sure no one dies up here on Titan's frozen tundra—but she certainly doesn't have a way with people. If she's like this with everyone, then I wonder how the other scientists can even stand to work with her...*

She was still trying to puzzle out the Commander when the dinner chime sounded, making her realize she hadn't even washed up in her private bathroom. On the way out, she quickly registered the nicely done painting of a T-Rex skeleton on one wall, but froze when she spotted the black and white photograph on the other.

It was some kind of dark mass that looked like it had been trapped in a lighter material—limestone, maybe? What the dark mass was, though, she couldn't make out. *Intriguing.* She would've spent more time on this mystery, but her rumbling stomach reminded her it was time for dinner.

2: Introductions

Kaden pealed repeatedly on Stria's doorbell—he was sure she'd heard the dinner chime, too, but he hadn't seen her in the hallway. Not that she couldn't have gone to the dining room a little early, but...he felt the need to go check on her, just in case. It never occurred to him that she might resent his assumption that she couldn't take care of herself.

"Dr. Reese!" *Probably shouldn't have sounded so surprised to see her...I am standing in front of her door, after all.*

"You look nice in blue," he blurted, trying to cover up the fact that he'd been distracted by the way her light blue eyes perfectly matched her uniform. *Idiot,* he scolded himself. *She'll never take me seriously as a scientist saying stupid stuff like that.*

"Kaden," she smiled, "please call me Stria. I always feel pretentious calling everyone by their title instead of their name. A little less human, somehow. And today of all days, I need to feel human."

"All right—Stria. Would you do me the honor of joining me for dinner?" he asked theatrically, bowing so low that his head nearly touched the smoke gray floor.

"Why certainly, sir," Stria agreed, laughing in spite of herself.

Kaden really looked like a scarecrow come to life, especially in his pale brown uniform. Add in his unruly thatch of straw-colored hair and dark eyes, and the effect was perfect.

"So where is it?" he asked, bewildered.

"The dining room?"

"Yes—I'm afraid I was so interested in everything going on around us earlier today that I didn't pay much attention to the words that were coming out of our esteemed Commander's mouth," Kaden added irreverently.

"If you squint hard enough, you can see the entrance through the glass walls of the science labs. Follow me, good sir—I'll get us there safely! It's pretty much impossible to get lost with this layout."

Thankfully. Stria winced slightly, but her companion didn't seem to notice.

"That stuffy military type must be the Assistant Commander, don't you think? He certainly seems self-important," Kaden whispered confidentially.

She looked at the man walking stiffly ahead of them in a deep green uniform. "I think his name was Astley or something," she whispered back, reveling in Kaden's closeness.

"Astley oh, Astley, you just walked past me," Kaden sang softly. He grinned widely, giving Stria a quick once-over. *It's astounding, really, what a change in hairstyle can do,* he thought, appreciating the way the loose strands fell around her face and neck, making her seem a little more approachable. Much more flattering than that messy braid she'd been working and reworking when they first arrived.

Blushing, she smiled gratefully. *I'm glad I'm with him instead of Ora.* Younger men weren't typically her style, but Kaden was different. Although they were probably no more than five or six years apart, she normally went for men a few years older than she was.

She sensed that Kaden's outlook on life couldn't be more different from hers—but maybe that's what she found attractive about him. He seemed to take life head-on as it came, while she was always trying to find ways to avoid the inevitable. Safety, not excitement, was her number one priority. And until now, she'd done a pretty good job of living up to that standard. But she couldn't deny that Kaden's presence made her feel a little bit better about being two billion miles away from home.

✫✫✫✫✫✫✫✫✫

The best strategy that Ora'd been able to come up with on her short walk to dinner was to try and monopolize the lead scientist's time as much as possible—he, of all people on this station, should know why she was here!

With that aim in mind, she rushed into the dining room—only to realize that she didn't know what he looked like, and he could be any one of the four men already seated. She was saved from her predicament when Dr. Kinney himself waved her over to an empty chair next to him.

"There's nothing formal about the dining arrangements here—any seat is available for any meal. They'll bring the food out to you, so no need for messy trays or conveyor belts. It's almost like being at an actual restaurant, except we don't get to pick from a menu. We're at their mercy when it comes to our meals," he explained with a wink, thoroughly enjoying his role as teacher.

"But I'm happy to inform you that they're good—both Ivy and Zevon graduated at the top of their classes in culinary school, or so I've been told. I'm Michael Kinney, by the way, lead scientist and station biologist. Michael—not Mike or Mickey or any variation thereof, mind you. You must be Dr. Amat—I've long admired your work. Your theories on the adaptive behaviors of Velociraptors were quite eye-opening."

He'd barely taken a breath during his monologue, rushing from one sentence to the next without waiting for Ora to respond.

Dr. Amat studied him carefully, taking in his slightly bewildered air, and began to have doubts about his ability to notice much beyond his own specialized area. His gray hair was disheveled, as if he'd run his hands through it one too many times.

He seemed to be missing his glasses, because once or twice he tried to push them up his nose and realized they weren't there, smiling sheepishly at her. She surmised that he wasn't really all that observant about human nature, or humans in general, and had a feeling that this serious man was the butt of more than a few jokes around the station.

He was the stereotypical absent-minded scientist—something

she'd rarely ever seen in real life. *Well, I guess it's good that I didn't come into this assignment expecting to make new friends,* Ora thought a little sadly. *Though it would've been nice to connect with **someone**.* She tried to push aside her now-familiar disappointment in the way her life was turning out and focus on dinner.

Aloud, she said, "Thank you, Dr. Kinney—it's always a pleasure to meet a fan of one's own work." *Well, that's true, at least,* she thought, trying hard to stay positive. *It's only the first day; it's bound to get better. After all, I haven't met everyone yet.*

"Yes, you'll find that we're quite well-versed in your research here on Titan. There are some very puzzling...ah...discoveries that we are eager to get your opinion on. Oh, let me introduce you to your fellow diners, by the way. And just in time since here comes Ivy with our dinner!"

Distracted, Dr. Kinney cut into the lasagna that had been placed before him. "Italian tonight—bravo! Thank you, Ivy."

Aside to Ora, he said, "We have various Earth-culture nights to switch things up from time to time. Our chefs make an extraordinary variety of foods for us here. My particular favorite is the curried jasmine rice with chicken. Delectable! I believe I was introducing you to the rest of the table?" Dr. Kinney rushed on around a forkful of lasagna.

Ivy, one of the aforementioned chefs, handed Ora her plate just as Dr. Kinney began his introductions. "I'm afraid we're over-represented by Americans right now. The group of scientists before us was a little more international. I believe there was a Russian, and a Brazilian, or possibly someone from Japan. I'm a little fuzzy on the details since they departed right before I arrived. Anyway, seated directly across from you," he said, pointing with another fork-load of lasagna, "is my assistant, Dr. Reid Everly."

"Hey, watch it with that fork, Michael—I've got my own lasagna, you know—I don't need yours, too! Nice to meet you, Dr. Amat," Reid said, almost as an afterthought, his pale, washed-out eyes focused on how dangerously close Michael's fork was to touching his own plate.

The old fool, Reid thought in annoyance. *If I have to sit within arm's length of him at one more meal, I'll...*

"And what do you do, Dr. Everly?" Ora asked politely, surprised at how tense the man was over something so trivial.

"I'm a microbiologist, and only Dr. Kinney's 'assistant' in so far as being the second in command of scientific operations on this station," he huffed, still watching the fork that Michael, for whatever reason, seemed in no hurry to move.

"Yes, yes, Reid, of course. I always forget how sensitive you are about the term 'assistant.' Let's go ahead and put that behind us, shall we? Anyway, next to him is Drake Galindo, one of our invaluable engineers."

"Leave Reid alone, Mike," Drake replied, purposely using the hated nickname. He never missed an opportunity to tease Dr. Kinney. He was an easy target and way too tightly wound, in Drake's opinion. Besides, it didn't hurt anything and was usually good for a few laughs.

"Must I remind you, Drake, that my name is Michael," he said, a new forkful of lasagna shaking with indignation, "though you should be addressing me as Dr. Kinney, if you want to address me at all."

Feeling vindicated by Drake's downcast look (not knowing he was hiding a smile at the good scientist's expense), he wrapped up the introductions.   "And finally, on my right is Kirby Yannick, our other, and far more pleasant, engineer."

"Nice to meet you, Dr. Amat," she said, suppressing a smile, her tawny eyes quietly laughing at the show they were putting on for Ora. "We've heard a great deal about you." Her wavy blonde hair had been pulled back, but several long strands had escaped and were threatening to dip themselves into her lemon ice. "Your first name is fairly unusual—does it mean anything?"

"Yes, it's from the Latin phrase 'ora pro nobis,' which means—"

"Pray for us," Dr. Kinney interrupted, eager to share his knowledge and unaware that he was being rude.

"Yes, that's right," Ora replied, grateful that she wasn't the only woman at the table.

Not that she wasn't used to being the only woman in the room on her teams back home—but this was a welcome change of pace. Kirby seemed capable and intelligent. *At least she's normal,* Ora thought with relief.

"Pray for us," Kirby echoed. "How fitting!" She laughed quietly then said again, "How fitting!" and would have gone on laughing into her plate of lasagna if Drake hadn't shot what seemed to be a warning glance in her direction.

Ok, so maybe she's not the most stable, Ora thought, soaking in the station's atmosphere. *Maybe after I've been here a while, I'll laugh at the wrong times, too. Though I sincerely hope not.*

Any further attempt at conversation died away immediately, as the others focused on eating the food in front of them. *So much for small talk,* Ora thought a little wistfully. On the plus side, it gave her a chance to process everything she'd seen and heard today.

But she fervently hoped every meal wasn't eaten in silence. She wasn't exactly an extrovert, but she did appreciate human interaction. And staring down at your own plate in silence didn't qualify in her book. *This could end up being a very lonely three years for me,* she thought sadly.

While Ivy was making the rounds at Ora's table, Zevon was busy serving Kaden's, which was set for six places, like her own. Ora recognized Commander Shan, and based on the uniform color, it looked like her assistant sat next to her. A lovely young woman with dark brown hair and a flattering turquoise uniform wandered in hesitantly and sat in the empty seat across from Kaden. The last table only had room for four people, but it was empty tonight.

Ora watched with interest as Kaden's attentions shifted from Stria to this lovely new addition to their party. *Probably going to cause some friction, that girl, without even realizing it,* Ora predicted, wondering if Kaden was going to end up creating some drama between the two women.

The one good thing about being in her 40s was not having to deal with all the romantic entanglements and heartaches of youth. She'd already been through that phase in her life and was glad it was over.

✫✫✫✫✫✫✫✫✫

"Zevon, sit, please! You've served everyone, now come sit down and eat your dinner," Jala urged in a motherly tone. Not that she was old enough to be anyone's mother on the station—at 45, she was one of the youngest station Commanders in the solar system. But she took a motherly interest in all her crew, knowing it was her job to keep them all safe. Obediently, Zevon joined the group.

"You must be our new scientists," he said, taking the last spot at the table and digging into his plate with gusto. One of the benefits of designing the menu was creating meals he actually wanted to eat!

"I'm Kaden, and this is Stria. Dr. Amat, I mean Ora, is sitting at the table behind us."

"Pleased to meet you both," said Zevon, gently shaking Stria's hand, and gripping Kaden's arm firmly.

"Zevon and Ivy are our pride and joy," Jala gushed. "It was a huge coup getting them assigned here instead of the Mars station. After all, if we're going to live so far from home, we may as well enjoy it, right? And there's nothing like good food to make the distance easier to tolerate."

Zevon laughed deeply and his dark eyes twinkled as he said, "I don't think you mind the distance at all, Jala. You're as happy as a clam up here, and I think you'd rather be on Titan than anywhere else in the galaxy." Jala readily agreed, her black eyes shining.

"It's true—I do love the adventure and strangeness of space. If I hadn't become an astronaut, I don't know what I would have done with myself!"

Stria shivered. She was nothing like Commander Shan. "How long have you been stran-I mean, stationed on Titan?" she asked, trying to keep the panic out of her voice. All this talk of how far away they were from home was making her anxious again.

"Hmm, well, let's see…Harris, how long have we been on the lug nut now? Six years?"

"No, seven!" the Assistant Commander piped up at Jala's elbow.

Although an astronaut like Jala, he had a military bearing about him, and his buzz-cut added to that impression. "Jala and I came here in 2093, and the station's crew joined us in 2094. That gave us a full year to run diagnostics, troubleshoot any issues, and work out all the kinks before the permanent station crew—that's the engineers, Misty Lee here, and Zevon and Ivy—came aboard. We had to make sure all the systems were working properly before we were willing to allow anyone else to risk their safety. If anything had gone wrong, we would've shut this station down immediately and come directly home. NASA would've been alerted to re-route the ships already heading toward Titan back to Earth."

"Luckily for us, everything worked with flying colors," Jala said proudly, "so we were able to host the first 3-year scientific mission in 2095. That first team left Titan in 2098, when Dr. Kinney and Dr. Everly came to relieve them. Their three years is up next year, so there will be some overlap when the next shuttle arrives to relieve them, since your three years won't be up yet. We think it's better that way." She and Harris exchanged a meaningful glance, and then Shan turned her attention back to her meal.

Stria was working out the timeline in her head. She, Kaden, and Ora had left Earth in 2093, arriving on Titan on October 23, 2100.

That meant that when Commander Shan and Assistant Adley arrived, she'd already begun her journey.

The final team was on its way now, only one year away from the Saturnian moon. If anything went wrong, would there be time to warn them? Stria tried to enjoy her meal, but the thought of being trapped on a space station so far from home, while everyone else joked casually about it, made it impossible.

She'd never been one to believe in premonitions or omens, but she felt uneasy about this place, and would be glad to leave as quickly as possible.

☆☆☆☆☆☆☆☆☆

"So, Misty Lee, what's your role on the station?" Kaden asked with great curiosity. She was absolutely stunning! He'd never met anyone who had truly gray eyes before—and he was already trying to think of excuses to spend time with her after dinner. Stria's quiet beauty had begun to fade from his mind already; oh, she was all right, of course, but Misty Lee was dazzling.

"I prefer to be called Misty...and I'm the cleaning lady," she said with laughter in her eyes and the hint of a Southern drawl.

"You're making fun of me," Kaden said, more attracted than ever.

"No, I mean it! I handle all the station's cleaning needs—and I have a small army of drones at my command. Makes me feel kind of powerful, actually. It's the first time in my life that a group of people depends on me, and if I wanted to go on strike, I could. Then the whole station would have to do whatever I wanted!" Her eyes twinkled merrily at Kaden.

"But you'd never do that! You're much too kind—I can tell by your eyes."

"Can you? I think that's a pretty stupid thing to say," she said, her smile fading a little. "You can only tell what people are like by getting to know them. And you don't know anything about me except the superficial facts of how I look and my role on the station."

"Touché!" Kaden laughed, thoroughly enjoying Misty's fiery responses. This was a woman he'd certainly like to know better. He thought he had a pretty good shot—he was closer to her age than anyone else on the station, and they'd be in close quarters for the next three years. Unless...

"You're not leaving when the next shuttle arrives, too, are you?"

"No, silly, the permanent crew (that's me!) stays for the full ten-year period. I won't leave until 2104, so I've still got four years. Although I have to say, I'm really going to miss it here. I never thought I'd like Titan so much. We kept hoping that NASA would renew our charter for another ten years, but..." she trailed off glumly, looking out at Saturn hovering protectively in Titan's hazy sky.

Kaden warmly said, "Then tell me a little bit about yourself, Misty, so I **can** get to know you! Why do you love it so much? I'm excited about all the scientific prospects and everything there is to discover—but it can't be the same for you because you aren't conducting experiments or anything like that...I mean...it must feel pretty monotonous doing the same thing day after day, right?"

Kaden did his best to recover after seeing her look of dismay over the implication that, not being a scientist, she had nothing worthwhile to do on the space station.

Stria turned away, her cheeks flushed with jealousy. It was always the same, no matter where she went.

Sensing Stria's discomfort, Harris gallantly asked her a few questions about herself to get her mind off their companions. He was displeased with Kaden's behavior, too, but for different reasons. It was highly unprofessional for the visiting scientists to be hitting on his crew members. He might have to pull Dr. Meade aside later and have a little chat with him.

✫✫✫✫✫✫✫✫✫

Ivy and Zevon excused themselves from their respective tables, brought out the dessert trays and coffee service, and began cleaning up the main course dishes.

"You are welcome to stay here and eat dessert," Jala informed the newcomers, "or you can take dessert and coffee back to your rooms. There are chutes in each guest room for your used dishes, which will deposit them in the clean-up area for Misty.

"Some evenings we have game night in the dining room after dinner, but tonight is a free night, and you may find it's better to go to bed early after your first day. Or, if you feel so inclined, you can explore your new home a little more, though you've seen nearly everything there is to see already."

After watching Kaden flirt lightly with Misty all through dinner, Stria chose to head back to her room. She knew it was foolish to be jealous. After all, she'd only known Kaden for a few hours; they hadn't even trained together before the long flight here.

And, although the flight had taken them seven years, they'd all been sleeping in their cryo-cocoons, so that didn't really count. But she still couldn't help feeling a slight twinge of envy after watching his dinner exchange with Misty. She was always too much of a wallflower for men to stay interested in her for long. They quickly moved on to women with more vibrant, outgoing personalities.

Harris, misunderstanding the source of her distress, asked Stria if she needed an escort back to her room.

"I remember how disorienting everything was when I was new here myself, this alien sky and unfamiliar surroundings," he explained unnecessarily. "Although this place isn't huge, it can be easy to get turned around."

He realized he was babbling a little, but Jala had warned him that this one might be a runner, and he wasn't about to let that happen again.

Stria was embarrassed that he thought she was so unstable that she needed an escort to make it the short distance back to her room, but after being practically ignored at dinner, it was nice to have someone's attention, and she accepted his offer in spite of her pride.

Why can't he talk to me like a normal person, instead of acting like I'm a fragile piece of glass or something? Stria thought with irritation. *If only I were better at hiding my fears, I wouldn't be having this awkward conversation.*

"Oh, and we don't have any animals here," Harris rambled on, grasping a little. Small talk had never been his forte.

"Too much clean up and too many variables to consider—what if a bird flew into the bay and died? Or got sucked inside the ventilation system? Too many what ifs to deal with, so they settled for large potted plants instead. And the greenhouse, of course. Safer to keep all the non-human life relegated to various plant species." He trailed off self-consciously, and they walked the rest of the way in welcome silence.

Dropping his charge off at her door, the Assistant Commander waited outside until he heard the lock click into position before he felt comfortable walking away. As much as he loved being here, he was secretly looking forward to end-of-mission; he didn't know if he could handle losing any more scientists to the strange form of space sickness that made them want to run.

He knew it was even harder on Jala—she felt personally responsible each time someone met their untimely death in the moon's unforgiving environment. He disliked keeping this information from the newer arrivals (even Reid and Dr. Kinney didn't really know what had happened before they'd come), but he also agreed with Jala that there was no sense in putting ideas into people's heads.

He would never forgive himself if his unguarded talk turned someone else into a runner.

☆☆☆☆☆☆☆☆☆

Seeing her own table disband, Ora decided to take her dessert and follow Michael Kinney. She'd come up with a few questions for him during dinner and hoped there'd be a place they could talk without distractions, since he seemed to get so easily derailed. She wondered if his absent-mindedness would be a hindrance to her work here.

"Dr. Kinney, a moment, please," she said hurriedly, catching him at the door. "I'd like to ask you a little more about your work on the station. Is there a quiet place we could talk?"

Always pleased when someone wanted to discuss his research, Dr. Kinney suggested the small library—it was more of a reading nook than anything else, but there were two bench seats covered by comfortable cushions and a small table on which they could place their dessert plates and coffee cups.

"Now, Dr. Amat, what would you like to know?" he asked her once they were comfortably seated. Ora made sure the door was tightly closed before asking the one question that had been on her mind since she'd been recruited back on Earth.

"Why am I here?"

3: Threats

"Kirby, just a second," Drake urged, recalling his fellow engineer to the dining room. "Why don't we take a stroll through the greenhouse and walk off our dinner?"

"Is this your weird way of saying you want to talk? Fine...let's go." She shrugged her shoulders, not caring who overheard.

Drake took her by the elbow, nervously guiding her the short distance to the greenhouse. *That's all we need, for someone to start asking questions,* he thought anxiously.

He fervently hoped no one had thought Kirby's behavior at dinner was odd.

"Thank you," he said curtly. "You know," he continued in a lighter tone, "even though we've been on this station for six years now, I still can't get used to the fact that sunset only happens every sixteen days. I keep expecting to wake up in the morning and see the sunrise, and that at night, I'll see the sunset."

"I don't mind it," Kirby said restlessly, aware he wasn't really speaking to her. Of course, they could've had this private chat in one of their rooms, but then practically everyone else on the space station would have seen them. And Kirby being alone in a private room with Drake would create a lot more questions than meeting in the greenhouse would.

"Alright, we're in the greenhouse now, so what's up?" Kirby said, impatiently removing his large hand from her dove-gray uniform.

She hadn't fallen head over heels for his rugged good looks like most other women did, and it grated on him, even after all this time, that he had so little influence over her.

Locking the door silently, he whispered, "Just to be on the safe side, let's go all the way to the back, near the roses."

"Are you honestly worried someone's going to spy on us? Don't tell me you're going a little batty yourself!" she burst out, surprised by his attitude.

"Don't worry about me—I'm perfectly sane; but after your performance at dinner, I'm a little concerned about **you**. Listen, don't get any ideas in your head about telling the newcomers what happened. You know how Jala feels about that."

"Why do you think I'd tell them about that?" she said harshly, wrinkling her pale eyebrows in disgust.

"The look on your face at dinner when you heard what Dr. Amat's name meant—I thought you were going to have a nervous breakdown in front of her! And don't kid yourself that I'm the only one who noticed your nearly hysterical laughter. Thankfully, you managed to pull yourself together by the end of the meal."

"I thought it was ironic, that's all. 'Pray for us'....I haven't prayed to anyone for anything in my entire life, and never thought I needed to until I came up here."

Her eyes clouded over for a second in memory. Recalling herself to the present, she murmured in a more subdued tone, "Look, I haven't said anything for two years; I'm not going to say anything now."

"That's my girl."

Kirby bristled at what she considered to be Drake's ingrained chauvinism. Even after several years of working together in a small space, it still caught her off guard.

"We don't want the new arrivals getting any crazy ideas," he continued, unfazed. His nearly black eyes searched her face for confirmation.

"Neither do I! Do you think I want to find another dead body?" she exploded. "I wish I'd never found Dr. Kamura out there...I have nightmares about it all the time. Trust me, I'm not saying anything to anyone!" Her tawny eyes blazed in anger.

"Whoa, back down, tiger! I thought I should check in on you, that's all." Drake stepped back a little, arms up defensively. "I mean we haven't really talked about it since we found him. Do you honestly think I don't see his frozen, dead eyes every time I try to sleep? Just...watch what you say, that's all. There's no sense in creating panic up here."

"Drake, I get it. You don't have to keep pounding it in...I haven't even told anyone else on the permanent crew. It's our little secret—and Jala's—and I plan to keep it that way."

"I know it's hard," he softened, remembering again what that day had been like. "Sometimes I wonder if I'll be able to keep it together myself; but it won't be much longer, and then we'll be home...away from all this artificial nonsense. Jala's crazy if she thinks a few plants, some artwork, and good food can make us forget we're on another world. Take care of yourself," he added, running out of steam. "Don't you go darting out into Titan's vast unknowns—I can't keep this whole station running by myself, you know."

"Oh, Drake...don't be so melodramatic!" Kirby scolded, an angry line forming along her forehead. "I'll be fine—and so will you."

She angrily pushed past him, leaving Drake alone in a maze of bright red roses.

He didn't hear her snap the door shut; he was reliving the horrifying morning they'd found the physician's frozen body lying right outside the station's emergency airlock.

*They shouldn't have done this to us. Someone should have stopped those Earth-bound experimenters before it got to this point. Sure, they'd done some preliminary studies that said humans would do fine for prolonged periods in space...but they never had to live it. I'd like to see **them** arrive on Titan and have to live here for a few years. I bet their precious studies would've turned out a little differently then.*

He broke off the nearest rose and crushed the red flower in his fist before grimly walking to his room.

✯✯✯✯✯✯✯✯✯

Before heading to his own quarters, Harris returned to the dining room to check on that foolish, young Dr. Meade and see to it that he wasn't making a nuisance of himself with Misty Lee.

Catching the Assistant Commander's eye as he poked his head in, Misty excused herself. "I get up pretty early to start on all my chores," she explained to Kaden, "so I really should head off to bed now. It was nice to meet you, and I do hope you find what you're looking for on Titan," she said sincerely.

Nodding to Harris, who was pretending to get another cup of coffee, she wandered to her room, thinking that Kaden wasn't too bad for a scientist. Most of them looked down on her because she didn't have a college degree—how could she! She was only 18 when she took the journey to Titan.

Almost everyone who came up here to do research had been blessed with rich parents and never had to worry about money in their entire lives.

Misty had to work all through high school to provide extra money for her family so they'd have food on the table. One of the main reasons she took this job was because of how much money it would bring her family. The people on this station couldn't understand that—even some of her crewmates struggled to understand what that was like.

Kaden's genuine interest in her, not as a specimen or a social experiment, was a breath of fresh air. Too bad he was only temporary.

✫✫✫✫✫✫✫✫✫

"Dr. Meade—a word, please," Harris demanded once Misty was out of sight.

Stirring his coffee slowly, he gruffly said, "I think you should know that we don't encourage romantic relationships on this station. It makes a mess of things, what with the tight living quarters, temporary assignments, and then the whole aging/not-aging thing. It's awkward when one of you leaves and doesn't age for seven years on the flight home, while the one who stays here continues to get older. It doesn't work out the way you think it will. So whatever romantic notions you're entertaining in that childish, fantasy world of yours—kill them off. I think it would be in your best interest, and Misty's, to discontinue all contact from this point forward."

"Hold on there, Adley," Kaden bristled. "Aren't you jumping to some pretty big conclusions? Who said I was interested in her? She's just...easy to talk to, that's all. I'm not looking to get involved with anyone right now! And besides, even if I was, what's it to you? Maybe you were in charge of a whole bunch of people back on Earth, but I report to NASA, not you. If she wants to spend time with me, I'm not going to turn her down."

Kaden could feel his face getting hot at the very idea that Adley could have some kind of control over his life on the station. He didn't sign up for this mission to be micromanaged and hounded over every little conversation.

"You're being extremely unwise, Dr. Meade."

"So are you—I don't take kindly to threats."

"Stand down, son...no one is threatening you, just offering you a little friendly advice learned the hard way."

Turning his back on the Assistant Commander, Kaden stalked sullenly back to his room, not waiting to hear what else Harris might've had to say. He'd heard enough already. Were these people prisoners here, or what? Whatever was going on, he didn't think he liked it.

Maybe things weren't quite as wonderful on the space station as they wanted the newcomers to believe.

☆☆☆☆☆☆☆☆☆

It was nearly midnight Earth-time as Ora stepped shakily out of the library. She had too much on her mind to wait for Dr. Kinney to make his plodding way to the door, and she welcomed the soothing silence of the empty corridors.

Well, not quite empty. Ora was so absorbed in her thoughts that she didn't notice the figure crouched behind the giant palm tree a few steps away. And neither did Michael until the stealthy figure quietly snuck up behind him and silently snapped his neck.

It was a risky move, but it was much safer than letting him live. Who knew what he'd been telling Ora, or would be telling her if he got the chance? Now he never would.

Quickly scanning the deserted hallway (deserted except for Ora's retreating form), the shadowy figure dragged Michael's limp body into the reading nook, then artfully arranged several books as if Michael had simply tried to reach one on a high shelf and fallen backwards.

Not my best work, but it'll have to do, the figure thought, closing the door carefully.

Jala Shan, conducting her nightly security sweep of the space station's corridors, saw nothing out of the ordinary, and heard only the gentle swish of Ora's door closing at the far end of the hallway.

4: A Sleepless Night

She could hardly believe what Dr. Kinney had been telling her, and now that she was back in her room, it hadn't completely sunk in.

Ora was still half-way convinced he'd been mistaken. *After all, he's not an actual paleontologist,* she thought with frustration.

According to Dr. Kinney, they'd collected several specimens for her to examine. Still, she highly doubted any of them were fossils.

With these new avenues of thought, Dr. Amat carefully re-examined the black and white photograph hanging on her wall. Dr. Kinney swore that had been taken here on Titan.

If she squinted hard enough, she thought she could make out the outline of something a little...spine-like, perhaps? Rationally, she knew it was her imagination taking an unfamiliar image and filling in the gaps to turn it into something she recognized.

Though if she turned the photograph just so, it did look slightly like...no. It was her mind playing tricks on her. But now that she'd imagined it, she couldn't stop seeing the image of a fossilized eel-like Phoebodus staring back at her from the photo.

Everyone knew there'd never been any life on Titan—maybe micro-organisms, but definitely nothing large enough to be seen with the naked eye. She wouldn't believe it until she had proof.

This image was probably nothing more than chunks of ice frozen into a dark mass of supercooled petroleum.

Dr. Kinney must've discovered some unusually shaped ice formations, or a frozen hydrocarbon stew that had never been alive at all.

☆☆☆☆☆☆☆☆☆

Stria tossed and turned, but sleep wasn't coming. She didn't want to admit it, but she was a little afraid of having to go back outside and start her actual work here. Inside the station she could pretend (almost) that she was on Earth, but out there—that wouldn't be possible. Not with Saturn overhead and the dirty orange atmosphere surrounding her.

She tried to focus on the interesting aspects of her work that had brought her out here...wave patterns in the seas, or Mares, as they called them on the moon. She didn't know why they always had to reach back into Greek and Roman mythology to name landscape features on alien worlds. *Don't we have enough names in modern history to choose from?* she thought restlessly, renaming them Lake Telluride and Loveland Sea to make herself feel better.

And there was a fascinating possible erosion and re-building phenomenon happening in one of the lakes that she wanted to examine for herself—the "Magic Island" they called it.

She'd been told that Drake and Kirby had created a special boat using the same hydrocarbon polymer that had been used on the rovers. That was something she could look forward to, being the first sailor on Titan—though she didn't trust this moon enough yet to want to be out on the "water" alone.

She had to keep reminding herself it was a sea made of hyper-cooled ethane and methane, not water. Any part of her suit that accidentally got wet would freeze solid in an instant. And if she fell overboard, she'd be dead before anyone could pull her out.

Maybe the Assistant Commander would be able to come with her. She wondered if she should call him Harris. It **was** his first name, after all, but he seemed so formal, she doubted that would be okay. It was such a mouthful to have to say 'Assistant Commander Adley' all the time, though.

Whatever she called him, his large, athletic frame and commanding demeanor made her feel like she'd be safe with him, wherever her research took her on this God-forsaken moon.

She'd have to ask Commander Shan's permission for him to accompany her on trips outside the station. Surely they did that for safety anyway, right?

As her mind roiled with these thoughts, a sudden chill raced along her spine, warning her that something wasn't right somewhere in the world—or, moon. She glanced at the clock: half-past midnight, Earth time.

I'm just imagining things, she told herself crossly, squeezing her eyes tight and trying to go to sleep.

✫✫✫✫✫✫✫✫✫

Back in his own quarters after a less-than-successful chat with Kaden, Harris Adley was thinking about the woman he'd left back on Earth—before he gave his life away to Saturn's largest moon.

She'd been so excited for him when he'd been chosen for this mission—it was the culmination of years of training and study, and he was grateful for the opportunity. She promised to wait for him until he came home, but...well, it hadn't been fair to even ask her—he realized that now. In all the pre-mission preparations he'd tried to forget about the age-gap issue, not wanting to remember that while he'd be sleeping peacefully during the seven-year journey and not aging a day, she'd get seven years older.

After video-comming her the first chance he got on arrival, it was a shock to see that instead of the vibrant 30-year-old fiancée he'd left behind, he was looking into the face of a 37-year-old with crow's feet that he didn't know anymore. Her life had continued moving forward while his had been suspended in a sleep chamber.

And when he returned to Earth, she'd age another seven years during his journey home, while he didn't age at all. It hadn't been right—asking her to keep on aging like that and losing whole decades of her life waiting for him to return. Even though his mission would be coming to an end in four years, it was already too late for them.

It had been during their second, awkward video-comm that same week—after they'd both worked through the painful implications of the age-gap issue—that they'd sadly agreed to end their engagement. He wanted her to be free to marry someone else and have children, something she'd always wanted, instead of having to put her life on hold for him until she was 55, when he returned to Earth.

He never commed her again after that—it had been too hard on them both and he wanted her to have a firm break, to get the chance to scrub her heart of every trace of him and find someone who was as Earth-bound as she was. That wouldn't be possible if he kept in touch with her.

He carefully folded her picture—the one he'd taken of her the day before he left—back into its special pocket in his uniform. He'd never told anyone about the photo, or the woman; it was too painful to put into words.

But sometimes, when the Sun shone especially bright through the Titanean haze, he took out her picture, talked to her a little about everything that had been going on, and kissed the face he remembered before stowing it safely back in his pocket.

If only he'd known the true cost of this journey ahead of time, maybe he wouldn't have come.

☆☆☆☆☆☆☆☆☆

Commander Shan undid the tight bun she always wore when she was on duty, picked up the book she'd been reading, and tried to relax. All she could think about, however, was the disruption the new arrivals were already causing to her beautiful schedule, and put the book back, unread, on her nightstand.

She rubbed her temples, trying to massage away the headache that was coming on. Tomorrow was going to be another long day—she'd have to show the new batch of scientists how to safely navigate life on this moon, making sure no one accidentally killed themselves on their first full day of work. **Babysitting.** Her least favorite part of this job.

Truth be told, she could do without the scientists altogether. They'd brought nothing but trouble from the first mission to now. Not only because of the runners, but because there always seemed to be someone who wanted to buck the rules—not realizing they'd been put in place for their own protection.

Why is it so hard for these people to understand that they're not on Earth? After all, that's why they came in the first place—to study something "alien" and "foreign."

Jala'd lived here long enough by now to consider this more her home than Earth, and no longer felt like an intruder on an alien world, unlike the awestruck scientists who rotated through on a regular basis.

In spite of their desire to be on a new world making new discoveries, the visiting scientists couldn't seem to get it through their heads that they had to be careful out in this landscape. It was as different from Earth as two worlds could possibly be!

They could never seem to fathom the potential dangers because their minds were too full of their research. Drilling this hole and cutting that slab, poking here, prodding there, not worrying about waking anything that still lived here, or about causing ecological damage. Anything for research's sake—even risking their lives!

Her mind went back to Dr. Jorgensen. *What a fool that one had been!* He'd been here a few years ago studying Titan's volcanoes, and had somehow managed to start an avalanche that took down half the mountain he was working on.

The vulcanologist had managed to bury himself under several feet of rock-hard ice when the mountain fell apart, and it took Harris and Jala three hours to free him. And he didn't even thank them for rescuing him! Instead, he kept congratulating **himself** on what a fantastic discovery he'd made regarding the volcano's composition! Jala'd been happy to see him go.

Her thoughts returned to the new arrivals. Kaden, she liked already. Jala didn't think she was going to get along with Ora very well—maybe they were too much alike, hard-headed and stubborn. Stria was a worry, though. She could sense the fear in that young woman the moment she stepped off the shuttle.

She'd have to tell Harris to keep a watchful eye on her, just in case. It wouldn't do for the pretty new scientist to fall into one of the Mares during her time here. With that settled, Jala rolled over on her side and promptly fell into an untroubled sleep.

5: First Assignments

D r. Reid Everly woke up with a headache. He hadn't slept well, trying to size up the new crop of scientists in his head, and kept reliving the humiliation of being introduced to Dr. Amat as Michael's assistant. As if he ran around getting Michael's coffee and supplies, following him around like some kind of underling!

*Good grief, what a ridiculous idea! I'm a microbiologist for God's sake—not some brain-dead secretary. Who does that man think he is? After two years here he still doesn't recognize how groundbreaking my work has been! Why, I've proven that there's actually life currently residing on Titan! Real, living microbes— we've never found anything like that anywhere else in the Universe. I've proven that life **currently** exists **here**!*

Even more remarkable considering they don't breathe oxygen and use the hydrocarbons around them as both air and food...Does the man have no humility? He hasn't even been able to complete half of his own experiments due to equipment failures! If I could've shoved him on that shuttle that brought the other three here yesterday and sent him back to Earth, I would have.

Taking a deep, steadying breath, Dr. Everly slowly got out of bed, kneeled down on the straw mat by his bedside table, and tried to meditate. *Breathe in, breathe out. Think no thoughts, be calm and relax.* After a few minutes, he felt peaceful enough to get dressed and join the others for breakfast.

It's only one more year, he reminded himself in front of the mirror, *and then we return to Earth. I, for one, am ready to be done with this place. No more thick, monotonous haze, no more Michael Kinney, no more walking around this giant lug nut. I almost feel sorry for the newcomers—they have no idea how hard the next three years are going to be. At least I'm almost out of here.*

Smiling to himself, he calmly walked to the dining room for breakfast.

"Good morning, Reid! I hope you didn't let Mike get to you last night," Drake offered apologetically as he walked into the dining room with Dr. Everly. "You know that he likes to get little jabs in here and there—probably jealous that you've gotten so much more to show from your time here than he has."

"It's ok, I'm used to it...I just wish that it wasn't the first impression he gave of me to Dr. Amat, that's all."

"She seems pretty shrewd—I wouldn't worry about her getting the wrong idea. I'd be more worried about her getting the right idea, if you know what I mean!"

Drake winked, but the gesture was lost on Reid.

"What do you mean by that?" Dr. Everly asked, the irritation he'd woken up with creeping into his voice.

"It was a bad joke on my part, sorry," Drake said sheepishly.

Seeing that Dr. Kinney's usual seat was still open, and that there was an open spot next to Commander Shan, Drake hurried on.

"Not to leave you to the wolves, but I don't think I can take Mike this morning. I really don't know how you've managed to stay sane these last two years after working so closely with that man!"

As the words slipped off his tongue, Drake's step faltered a bit, causing Commander Shan to steady his elbow as he reached for the chair next to her. *What if Reid...? No, he wouldn't—not after all this time. He couldn't.*

"You ok this morning, Drake?" Jala asked with genuine concern.

She liked Drake in spite of his playboy façade. She knew that act had worn thin with Kirby—maybe it would have with her, too, if she had to work as closely with him as Kirby did. But Jala liked him all the same. He was upfront and didn't mask what he was thinking. She wished more people were like that.

"I'm ok, I just wasn't paying attention to where I was going, that's all." *I wonder if Kirby ever considered Dr. Everly...maybe I should ask her about it. But two trips to the greenhouse in two days might seem a little too coincidental.*

✫✫✫✫✫✫✫✫

Cleaning up after breakfast, Ivy mentioned how odd it was that

Michael had missed his morning meal.

"That's not like him, Zevon," she fretted.

"Mike's probably just too busy chasing down some new scientific mystery—you know how he gets when he's on the verge of a breakthrough."

She sighed wearily. "I guess so," she admitted, but couldn't shake the unpleasant feeling that something was wrong.

★★★★★★★★★

Gathering the new arrivals in one of the science labs after breakfast, Commander Shan and Assistant Commander Adley went over the types of equipment available to the scientists, and the various instruments at their disposal. For anyone else, it would've been a dry and boring lecture. But for the new scientists, it was a different story.

"Is that a laser ablation system?" interrupted Kaden. "I can't believe it—I kept trying to get my hands on one of these back on Earth but was never able to!" His face broke into a broad grin in spite of Adley's presence.

"Yes, you'll find we have the most up-to-date equipment, analysis tools, and software systems to allow you to perform your work at the highest levels. Now, as the Commander was saying..." Harris interjected in an attempt to reign in Dr. Meade's enthusiasm. *This young man keeps finding new ways to annoy me,* he thought irritably.

"Thank you, Harris. Yes, the labs are incredible, I assure you," continued Jala. "However, there are some very crucial things to learn about working on Titan, and your lives could depend on how well you pay attention today."

Ora's mind had been wandering up until now. She, too, had been quite impressed with the expense taken to get these fine instruments on the station. She had several radiometric dating devices available to her, along with a pneumatic air scribe—which was quite unusual considering there shouldn't even be fossils to clean and examine here. At the mention of life or death, though, she forced herself to pay attention to the Commander.

Leading the group into the supply room attached to the small exam room, the Commander showed them where the Terratents were stored. She pulled one from its sealed pack and demonstrated how to inflate the tent and ensure that all the seams and seals were airtight from the inside.

Harris gave a very thorough presentation on how to work the thermal regulation, filtration, and purification systems.

"These tents are your station-away-from-station," he droned. "They'll provide you with breathable air, protection from surface contaminants and, thanks to the thermal regulators, a warm place to eat or sleep during a long expedition or a sudden storm. Each tent can house up to three people if necessary."

"If you get stuck in a rainstorm, your best bet is to set up a Terratent and stay put. We're not about to let you all wander aimlessly around the moon in the thick, inky torrential rains that made everything black and sticky, covering visors and vehicles in a matter of minutes.

"Another thing we pride ourselves on is that no one goes out alone—ever," Harris added, looking hard at each scientist in turn.

"Those who've been foolish enough to pursue some special project of their own have only ended up getting stranded and needing one of us to come rescue them. It's unwise, and it's an unnecessary risk to take. Don't do it. Go out in pairs at a minimum. The Commander and I can't guarantee that we'll always be available to travel with you to the various experiment locations on the moon, however.

"I know that you, Dr. Meade, will be eager to get a look at the sand dunes near the equator—that's a half-day's journey from here, a minimum of two days away from the station. The Commander and I can't afford to be away from the lug nut for that long, so one of your fellow scientists will have to accompany you."

"What about trips to Kraken Mare and Ligeia Mare?" Stria asked in a strained voice, worried that she might be told Harris Adley couldn't go with her. His military bearing made her feel like he would be a lot more useful in a bad situation than any of her fellow scientists; she really didn't want her life to depend on Kaden or Ora.

"Those are close enough that one of us could make the quick trip out and back with you," Jala said. "It's only an hour from here to the Mares, and as long as you could wrap up your experiments within a day, we could spare the time."

Stria tried not to show her intense relief, but the Assistant Commander noted that her shoulders relaxed slightly with the news. He wasn't about to let her go wandering around by herself anyway—she might not come back!

"So, Kaden, it sounds like you'll need to travel with one of us scientists for your more far-reaching experiments," Ora said. "I don't mind joining you on a few treks—there are some far-flung parts of the moon I need to explore, too."

"Delighted," he said genuinely. He'd been impressed with Ora the few times they'd interacted since being here. She wasn't afraid of whatever they might encounter, and she seemed genuinely interested in exploring their temporary home.

Unlike Stria, who, Kaden had to admit, was turning out to be a bit of a let-down. Why, she even seemed scared to leave the station! He thought the psych tests they all went through weeded out people like that. She might be pretty, but she was practically scared of her own shadow, and it wasn't attractive to him.

Not that he was here to be attracted to anyone. He was totally focused on his work. Absolutely. No woman was going to distract him from the big things that were bound to come his way! Although Misty wasn't just any woman, and his mind wandered a bit when he remembered her piercing gray eyes.

After making everyone take a turn operating the Terratent, and feeling satisfied that even Stria would be able to figure it out on her own if needed, Commander Shan led them all to the bay, where they quickly donned their space suits. With everyone properly suited up, Jala and the Assistant Commander gave them driving lessons with the rovers.

They'd need to know how to keep from capsizing on the ice boulders and be able to maneuver well enough to avoid the valleys, rifts, and minor cracks that could quickly open up into large chasms. The combination of low visibility and low gravity made driving on Titan a complicated dance that had to be mastered quickly.

A couple of scientists had nearly flipped their rover upside down a few years ago when they over-accelerated and drove up a steep embankment that had been hidden in the thick haze.

Finally, Jala taught them how to use the communicators in their space suits to call the station for help. "If you ever need help outside the station, switch over to band 6, which is the frequency for Harris or myself. You are each attuned to band 3. These are invaluable—do not damage them or you'll lose your ability to communicate outside the station. Remember, the rovers do not have communicators in them—only your suits."

"No one can hear you scream without them," Ora whispered quietly to Stria. She knew she shouldn't—but it was far too easy to tease her colleague. Kaden, not hearing what Ora said, saw Stria's face go white and said quickly, "So, when do we get to start working on our individual—or group, as the case may be— experiments?"

"Actually, this afternoon," Harris replied in his military monotone.

"After lunch, you'll each be given a list of assigned experiments for the next month. These assignments come from NASA and a coalition of other space agencies, with varying priority levels to each project. You're free to choose which experiments to do when, as long as all of the experiments are completed by the end of each month.

"Jala communicates regularly with Earth and updates them on the status of various experiments. She also includes any results or highlights that you pass along to us. If you find something particularly exciting, let us know and it will be relayed to NASA. In some months you'll have free reign to conduct whatever additional experiments or investigations you would like—we don't like to have things too regimented. This way, you have the freedom to pursue any sidelines that are of interest to you, while also having specific goals to meet in order to feel productive."

"And what do Michael and Reid do while we're out trying our wings?" asked Kaden, pleased that they'd have lots of things to work on, and yet still have the opportunity to go down rabbit trails if they wanted.

"Oh, they also have assignments they're working on, the same as you do," Harris explained in a business-like tone. "Sometimes the assignments may require field work, and sometimes you'll be relegated to lab work or to reviewing data from previously conducted experiments. You should find plenty to keep you busy here if you **want** to be busy."

His brusque attitude made them all feel as though they'd better be busily engaged in work whenever they saw him.

✫✫✫✫✫✫✫✫✫

Lunch was a quick affair since everyone had their various tasks to complete afterward, but Michael's absence at a second meal didn't go unnoticed.

Reid was grateful to be free from Michael's condescension for a change, while Ivy noted once again to her fellow chef how concerned she was that he failed to show at lunch. She made him promise that if Michael missed dinner, too, Zevon would take a special plate to his room and make sure the older man was alright.

Ora was slightly surprised not to see Michael at all today after their conversation last night, but then again, maybe she shouldn't be. After all, he was more than a little absent-minded at dinner yesterday, and she wouldn't be shocked if he regularly missed meals because he was too focused on his own work to notice he was hungry.

Misty and Kaden didn't notice much but each other, while Jala and Harris had too many notes to compare after the morning's training to worry about a rogue scientist.

☆☆☆☆☆☆☆☆☆

Lunch ended much too quickly in Stria's mind, and she was reluctantly receiving her individual assignment sheet from Harris.

After the new scientists had their marching orders for the month, he was happily heading off to more enjoyable duties when Jala quietly stopped him.

"I may need you here a bit longer," she whispered enigmatically, and he obediently waited by Jala's side for further instruction.

Stria saw that her first assignment was taking samples from Kraken Mare. She was to gather some of the sea itself, bits of the "shoreline," and photograph various features up-close. If there was time today, she was also supposed to manually operate a submersible probe that captured temperature, pressure, and liquid composition. The probe was equipped with a camera and high-intensity light to search for anything interesting in the Mare's liquid-natural gas depths, though Stria doubted there was anything to see.

She knew there wasn't any life here—not anything large enough to see through a camera lens, anyway, but she was glad for the direction. She'd been worried about having too much free time to think, but in reviewing her assignment list, she was relieved to see there were so many tasks to accomplish that she'd have very little time for anything but work and sleep over the next month. She was eternally grateful to the scientists back on Earth who had so carefully planned out her time.

Later, maybe she'd be brave enough to try out the boat and see how far she could go into the Mare itself, but for now, sticking close to the shoreline and letting a probe do the work for her was more than enough.

✫✫✫✫✫✫✫✫✫

Much to Ora's satisfaction, she had several assignments over the next month related to investigating the items of interest that had already been found. It seemed that all of the suspected "fossils" had been unearthed during construction of the various supply sheds placed around the moon. Titan Station Zero was the main base of operations, but according to the map that was included with her assignment list, there were several smaller outposts scattered across the moon's surface that would also require her attention.

Much of her work today would be focused here at the station and involve reviewing data with Michael. That was fine with her. Contrary to worrying about how she'd fill her time here, she was now worried about having enough time to examine everything.

What a tragedy to have to turn her research over to someone else if she really did find anything worth writing home about. If that happened, maybe she'd request to stay on and leave the station with the last group of scientists.

✫✫✫✫✫✫✫✫✫

Kaden was disappointed to see that his trips to the dunes and some of the more far-flung locations on the moon were not included in the list of assignments for his first month. Instead, he was going to be sticking closer to the base: taking samples of the area between Kraken and Ligeia Mare and multiple external samples around the station.

He was also going to be drilling deep into the moon's surface from multiple areas all within walking distance of the station, which weren't as exciting to him as exploring the more distant cryovolcanoes and alluvial plains. *Oh, well.* He was sure he'd get to tackle those things over the next three years. *It's only my first day on the job, after all. Might as well start small and then work up to the big stuff.*

"Before you all break off, you must inform Assistant Commander Adley or me where you'll be working for the day. We like to know how many people are outside the station at any given time. Avoids surprises that way," Commander Shan explained cryptically, revealing nothing in her carefully blank expression.

Kaden was determined to get outside and walk around. He came here to experience the majesty and uniqueness of Titan, not stay inside a building all the time. Besides, he wanted to get those boring deep core samples over with as soon as possible.

Ora was going to stay in and compare notes with Dr. Kinney, and Stria timidly asked if Assistant Commander Adley would be able to accompany her to the lake, as most of her assignments for the month required her to be outside the station.

"Ok, so that's Dr. Meade, Dr. Reese, and Harris outside the

station. If I don't see you at dinner, you'll hear me hail you on your communicators. Good luck," she added, giving Harris a weighty glance. After several years of working together, he could read her glances pretty well. "Keep an eye on her and both of you come back safe," was what he understood that look to mean.

Once released, Ora hurried off in search of the other two scientists staying in today. Dr. Kinney had promised her she'd get to examine one of their more interesting finds and she felt she'd already wasted too much time as it was. Not that it was going to be an actual fossil—she was sure of that.

But she was willing to suspend her disbelief for a few hours this afternoon and see what Dr. Kinney had been so excited to show her. Probably nothing more than a piece of space junk that had been captured by Titan's atmosphere—a stray meteor, possibly, or pieces of a runaway comet.

When Ora got to the lab, however, it was empty except for Dr. Everly, hunched over a tiny piece of equipment doing who-knows-what. She didn't want to disturb him, so she wandered off in search of the absent Dr. Kinney on her own.

6: Surprises

Stria was struggling to control Rover 6 on the way to Kraken Mare. In spite of her earlier lessons, she couldn't help but bounce the rover jerkily over every mound along the way.

She kept shooting quick looks at her passenger to see if he noticed how bad a student she'd been.

Harris was rarely fazed by anything as trivial as bumpy driving and, being focused entirely on navigating them to the Mare, barely registered how rough the ride was. He even congratulated Stria for bringing them safely to their destination in less than the usual hour. (45 minutes Earth-time, thank you very much.)

Setting up their Terratent (just in case), Harris kept a watchful eye on Stria as she neared the lake's shoreline. He'd been impressed by her grit in getting them here, but he remained uneasy about her on the whole. The skies were perfect (for Titan, anyway), and there didn't appear to be any rain looming on the horizon. They should have all the time in the world, er, moon, to get today's experiments completed in time to be home for dinner.

Making quick work of the shoreline and lake samples, and being quite brave about it all, too, Stria thought, she directed her attention to the probe. Harris had already gotten the screens together so they could watch in real-time as the probe took photos and video images of anything that might be below the lake's surface.

She quickly snapped a couple of test photos to check out the probe's camera.

"Oh, it's like looking right at the shoreline," Stria declared happily, making sure Harris took a look at the photos.

"See, right there—it looks like an alluvial flow—but there's no liquid there now. That seems to be calibrated correctly, so I think it's ready to put in the water—I mean, methane. Here goes nothing!" she said almost giddily, and shoved the weighty probe into the liquid, being extremely careful not to splash any on her space suit.

Guiding the probe through the surface methane from the control panel, she and Harris checked for any potential malfunctions before sending it diving below the visible part of the lake.

It was such absorbing work that Stria almost forgot she was afraid of this forbidding landscape, even noting once or twice the unusual ripple pattern ingrained into the pale ochre shoreline.

"Not sure what we're looking for," Harris said in his practical tones. "But if anything's there, we'll find it. Plenty of time to explore this side of the lake with the probe today."

"I don't expect we'll find much," Stria replied with certainty.

Although she should be excited—no one had ever seen beneath Kraken's Mare's dark surface before!—she couldn't help but feel they were wasting their time. Sure, the temperature and chemical analyses would be interesting to have, but they weren't actually going to see anything except the lake's dark liquid and the solid ice bottom (if the probe could even go that deep). It was foolish to even pretend life existed on the surface of this place, let alone in the depths of an inky, subzero methane lake.

"Looks like a radar signal's being picked up by the probe," Harris said, displacing her thoughts.

"That isn't possible," Stria said confidently, before noting the radar trail on the display. She stared in disbelief. "But that's nowhere near the bottom of the lake—at least, it shouldn't be!" *What's going on here?* she wondered.

"No visual yet—could be a glitch—you never know how these gadgets are going to react to the cold until it's too late. Why, I remember one scientist whose entire machine cracked wide open while it was supposed to be sampling the rain out here. Couldn't handle getting pummeled by 300-degrees-below-zero oil droplets."

Harris couldn't help but smile as he remembered the tantrum the little scientist threw when his precious machine fell apart. That one hadn't been very easy to work with. He hoped working with Stria would be much more pleasant. In a purely professional way, of course. She was much too fragile for anything else. And besides, he didn't form emotional attachments with the temps.

"Wait—I think I see...was that movement?" Stria squeaked

excitedly. "There, to the right edge of the screen—something a little lighter than the liquid around it. Did you see that?"

Harris strained to see around her bulky spacesuit, and got the tiniest glimpse of something that nearly knocked him off his feet.

"That...that almost looked like an eel—would you agree, Dr. Reese?" *Please tell me I'm not hallucinating; I can't afford to succumb to space sickness. Not out here. How would Dr. Reese make it back to the base?*

"Call me Stria, please, Harris. I think I saw it, too, but I can't be sure what it was. Something definitely moved past the camera, though. And it appeared to be self-propelled."

"Meaning?"

"Meaning that whatever it is, it's alive."

✮✮✮✮✮✮✮✮✮

Ivy and Zevon were gathering the ingredients for dinner—it was going to be one of Ivy's personal favorites tonight, mushroom polenta with grilled steak tips. It reminded her of New Orleans somehow. Not that she missed home that much anymore; after six years on the station she'd gotten over any homesickness long ago.

But sometimes it was nice to remember skies that changed colors, from blue to red to pink to yellow, and gray when it rained. Here it was just different shades of orange that she'd run out of names for. Not that seeing Saturn suspended in the sky wasn't breath-taking, it was, but...it wasn't quite the same.

"What are you thinking about so seriously, Ivy?" Zevon probed, noticing how unfocused her green eyes were. She went into these quiet phases every once in a while, and it made him worry about her. He'd heard about people going crazy in space, and he didn't want it to happen to Ivy. She was his rock on this frozen, peach smoothie of a moon, and sometimes he wondered what he'd do without her.

"Remembering the street vendors in New Orleans, that's all," she smiled absently. "I could almost smell the jambalaya and crawfish cooking. And the sounds—the sounds of all the traffic and people rushing past were so real. It was so lively. Sometimes it's nice to remember things, don't you think?" She looked up at his dark face, so warm and genuine.

"Nice and dangerous. That's how people have mental breakdowns up here...thinking too much about how nice everything was at home and how different everything is in space. And how much they want to go home but can't."

Ivy was ready to hurl a smart remark at him, but seeing the worry in his ebony eyes stopped her short. "I'm alright, Zevon. It actually helps me to think about Earth once in a while—brightens me up a little on my down days, you know? I promise to let you know if I start struggling with being here, ok? And you have to promise to let me know, too," she winked at him, trying to lighten the mood.

"As long as you're sure you're ok, Ivy..." He searched her intelligent face for any hint of trouble. Satisfied, he added, "Let's get that polenta together."

Walking past him with a basket of mushrooms they'd grown in the station's greenhouse, Ivy allowed her arm to graze his lower back. "You're a really good guy, Zevon."

One of the best, actually; better than any of the men I knew on Earth.

He bent his head and began furiously chopping scallions, hoping she hadn't seen his jaw drop in pleasant surprise. The smile in her voice always got to him. He was being ridiculous, and he knew it.

She hadn't accepted this assignment to find a boyfriend, and he hadn't come here for a relationship, either. He'd worked his tail off trying to stand out in the overcrowded restaurant business on Earth and hadn't gotten anywhere for his trouble. Chefs were a dime a dozen, and everyone believed they were the next big thing. It was hard to get any investor to take you seriously, even with a five-star rating under your belt.

This assignment was his way up the ladder—proving he could create a full menu on his own (well, with Ivy) and consistently serve excellent food to a station full of people for several years. When their assignment was over, he'd have enough money to open his own restaurant, serving many of the same dishes he'd perfected with Ivy.

It was the dream he'd been striving for his whole life, and having Ivy working by his side had made it all seem possible. But once they left the station, there was no guarantee they'd even live in the same country, let alone be working in the same kitchen. His dream wasn't as vivid and colorful without his co-chef. If he were totally honest, all of his dreams ended the same way—working alongside Ivy by day and going home with her at night.

Now I am being ridiculous, he thought. *She'd never go for something like that. At least I'll get to be up here with her for a little while longer.* One more group of scientists was scheduled to come next year for a final three-year mission. That gave him, what? Four more years with her? *Not nearly enough, but I'll take what I can get.*

He risked a glance in her direction, noting for the hundredth time how perfectly her wavy red hair complimented her eyes. He let his gaze wander slowly down to the slender fingers that were expertly julienning carrots for the slaw they'd serve on the side. One of her contributions to their shared menu. They made such a good team. What would he do without her?

"Now you're the one who's drifting off!" Ivy teased, realizing all of a sudden that her knife gliding against the cutting board was the only sound in the kitchen. She glanced at Zevon and he quickly got back to work, melting butter for the polenta. She had to admit, she was attracted to him. She shoved down the thought of how good it would feel to caress his neck and run her fingers through his thick, black hair and instead ran her fingers through the pile of freshly julienned carrots, tossing them in a light vinaigrette.

✫✫✫✫✫✫✫✫✫

They stared intently at the probe's video feed for another hour, but didn't see any other mysterious shapes drifting, floating, or swimming past the lens.

"We'd better start heading back to the station," Harris said reluctantly. "I'd hate for us to return too late for dinner. Besides, it doesn't look like there's much more we can accomplish today."

Stria, deeply shaken by the creature sighting, but doing her best not to show it, agreed readily. She hoped her eagerness to get back inside to the safety of the station wasn't too noticeable. She had no idea whether the mystery creature knew how to creep on land or not, but she wasn't willing to stick around and find out. Unfortunately, she'd have to come back tomorrow and search another section of the lake, no matter how nervous she was about encountering previously unidentified sea creatures.

This was her bread and butter, after all—studying seas and the life within them, no matter what part of the solar system they happened to be found in. She only hoped Harris would join her again tomorrow. His calm, steady presence was reassuring, and had kept her focused when her mind would've preferred to shrink back in panic.

Not that he was the type of company she normally kept. He was a little too rigid and regimented for her tastes. She didn't imagine that he could be considered an intellectual in any way. But he was a good guy to have around for grunt work, she supposed. And he was good at following orders. He'd done his job well today.

As she analyzed her companion, she was able to pack up the scientific instruments almost calmly, while Harris took down the Terratent. *I wonder if that thing is strong enough to withstand the sea creatures of Titan?* she fretted, hoping they'd never be in a position to find out.

She guided the probe back to shore and carefully lifted it into the carrier using the specialized gloves Harris had given her. It didn't appear to have been harmed in any way by its undersea adventure, so maybe they'd get a lot of good use out of it before the bitter cold finally worked its way inside the machine.

"I don't think we need to bring this to the Commander's attention," Harris deliberated, returning to their earlier conversation as if more than an hour hadn't already passed. "It seems to me like we need more evidence before we can confirm what we did or didn't see today. Until we have incontrovertible proof, I think it's best to say nothing."

Stria was slightly surprised that Harris would even know that word, let alone how to use it in a sentence. He'd only been through military training and hadn't even attempted to go to university. She felt the tiniest prick of conscience, wondering if maybe she'd been wrong to assume that he wasn't as intelligent as someone like her with a Doctorate in oceanography. *I guess I'm not above stereotyping,* she thought without irony, not realizing that was all she'd been doing from the moment she'd met him.

Aloud, she said, "I think you might be right—no need to get anyone's hopes up that there's anything living in these seas just yet. We'll have to come back tomorrow and try to find better evidence."

I can't believe I'm saying this. But I have to get used to being outside the station, I have to! I've got three years' worth of experiments to do and I can't do all of them indoors. And besides, I don't want to be thought of as the weak link for the rest of my time here.

Shivering slightly, she followed Harris back to the rover with the now-packed equipment, and thankfully, he offered to drive them back to the station. She wasn't sure she could handle another turn at the console after running them into and over every lumpy piece of ground on the way to the sea.

She closed her eyes as Harris engaged the rover's engine and began the long drive back to the station. She hoped he wasn't feeling talkative, because she had a lot she needed to think about on the return trip. She didn't like the wrestling-match she was having with her own conscience because of Harris Adley, and wondered for the first time if any of her assumptions about him were true.

★★★★★★★★

Ora'd finally given up her search for Dr. Kinney—she was just wasting time and was eager to review the samples with or without him.

Seeing Dr. Everly still hard at work in his own lab, she gently knocked on the door, unhappy at having to disturb him.

Even that light sound made the scientist jump out of his chair, nearly knocking the electron microscope he was looking through off the table.

"What do you want? Can't you see I'm busy?" he snarled, righting his chair and the microscope in one swift move.

"I can't find Dr. Kinney anywhere, and I need someone to give me access to those samples I'm supposed to be studying all month."

Ora looked back at him steadily and held her ground. She wasn't one to be intimidated by temper tantrums.

"Fine, third drawer on the right, two rows from the bottom. But you'll have to examine them in one of the other labs. This one is for **my** equipment."

Ora gladly agreed to let Reid have the lab to himself, and set herself up in the one furthest away from him. She could still see him, however, since those glass walls didn't offer anyone privacy.

Turning her back to him, she prepped the first sample and slid it under her own microscope, not hoping for much.

As she adjusted the magnification, swirls and circles began to emerge from the chaos. After a few more adjustments, Ora sat back and stared at the microscope, stunned.

So that's what Michael was so excited to show me!

Minute mollusks, shells intact, were suspended in the frozen goo of Titan. Whether they were still alive or merely fossils, she wasn't sure yet, but either way, this would rewrite everything humans knew about life in the Universe.

No wonder they wanted a paleontologist up here.

☆☆☆☆☆☆☆☆☆

Kaden was tired of drilling core samples around the base. He'd only managed to get three cores in three hours, and they were all monotonously similar, except for their depths. They varied between 500 and 1,000 feet. He was supposed to go all the way down to 2,000 feet today if his equipment could take the friction. This stuff was harder than anything he'd ever sampled on Earth.

He checked the time again. Only thirty minutes later than the last time. This was the most boring part of the job, and he hated it. But better to get it out of the way early on and focus on more interesting things during the rest of his time here. *Like Misty,* he thought, wondering what she was doing now. He had no intention of following Harris Adley's orders to stay away from her. She was the most exciting thing about this place!

Kaden almost wondered if the Assistant Commander was jealous.

He was probably old enough to be her father; after all, he had to be what, mid-40s? And Misty couldn't be more than 25...so a young father, but still old enough to Kaden. Well, she didn't seem to be interested in Adley, at least. *Not that I'm interested in Misty, either. It'd just be nice to have someone fun to talk to, that's all.*

He'd barely caught a glimpse of her this morning at breakfast. She was already finishing up her meal when he and all the rest of the scientists strolled in at seven a.m. He'd intended to grab the empty seat next to her, but Reid Everly pounced on him, and Kaden was forced to listen to the man drone endlessly on about the minute aspects of his research.

Some people don't know when to turn it off. Shop talk was fine on the clock, but Kaden didn't consider his meals to be on-the-clock. His evenings weren't supposed to be on the clock, either.

At least lunch had been better, and Harris had been too busy with Jala to interfere with him and Misty then.

The thought of Misty's beautiful gray eyes got him through the final tedious sample. "So, your parents named you after your eye color?" he'd joked at lunch. "Yes," she said, arching one dark eyebrow attractively, her look daring him to contradict her. He had to find a way to spend some time alone with her tonight. Purely as friends, of course.

He wasn't sure what he thought about the others yet, though.

Drake might be ok, but he seemed to spend all his non-working hours trying to flirt with Kirby or Ivy. Or, strangely enough, Commander Shan, who didn't really seem to be the flirtatious type. Not that Kaden didn't like her as a person, but...well, maybe she was a little **too** interested in making sure everyone was comfortable and having a good time.

It came off as a bit forced, but maybe she wasn't naturally a people-person. He tried to imagine an extreme introvert like Stria being in charge of a space station, and guessed she'd probably seem a little strange to newcomers, too.

Guiltily, he reminded himself that Stria wasn't terrible, once you got her mind off the fact that they were on a brave new world that she wasn't being very brave about. She **was** pretty reserved, though. He generally preferred women who didn't make getting to know them as boring as drilling core samples.

He pulled his thoughts back to the task at hand, which had proven to be harder than expected. His special hover cart had been equipped with diamond-tipped titanium blades to chop up the core samples into more manageable sizes, but even that powerful combination struggled to bite through the frozen ice layers.

At least it gave him time to think about Misty—er, the space station—and how cool it was to look up through the day's thin tangerine haze and see Saturn in all its glory. Finally finished, he bundled the core sections into their special deep-freeze compartments, and tossed them onto his robotic cart a little too powerfully. He still wasn't used to this weird gravity.

I hope the others had a more interesting first day than I did, he thought innocently, walking the short distance back to the lug nut, as the crew affectionately called the hexagonal station, with the little cart following cheerily behind him.

7: Unpleasant Discoveries

Misty was making her daily rounds, dropping off clean laundry for all the guest rooms. She felt like the station was a glorified hotel in many ways. Room service, a restaurant, and no one ever had to clean their own rooms if they didn't want to. Well, everyone except Misty, of course.

She'd developed a rhythm of working her way clockwise around the station from the laundry room at the northeast corner, and made a habit of watering the huge potted fruit trees and tropical plants along the way.

She even refreshed the linens in the empty rooms so they didn't get too musty waiting for their next tenants. Right now, there were three empty rooms before she got to the angle in the hexagon that meant Ora's gold-themed room was next.

She wasn't a fan of the monochromatic theme for each room.

Hers, for instance, had pale cream walls, and all the fabric was a shimmery jade green. She would've preferred something a little more neutral, like tan carpet, and wished the curtains weren't so dark. Or that at the very least that she could have chosen a multi-colored comforter. Even the towels were a matching shade of green.

But it was probably the only sure-fire way to keep from mixing everything up between the rooms. People were funny—they didn't want to use the same towels someone else had used the day before, even when they knew everything had been cleaned.

She passed the emergency airlock between Ora and Kaden's rooms, and placed a neat pile of clean tan linens on his matching comforter. She lingered a bit to see if he'd added any personal touches that would hint at his personality. Other than 'disorganized' she couldn't tell much.

His things probably haven't even come back from quarantine yet, silly. He couldn't have brought much with him anyway. They only allowed you a small duffle of things from home, including "off-duty" clothes that they never got to wear. In Commander Shan's mind, the only off-duty times were when you were asleep.

Sighing with disappointment, she moved on to Reid's chaotic jumble of a room, trying to find a place to put his clean laundry where it wouldn't be contaminated by the dirty clothes littered everywhere. She gingerly slid a pile of books away from the center of the bed, and tried not to think too hard about how they could've gotten so filthy, putting his clean bundle of laundry in the center. *There, he has to notice that!*

After a quick blast of sanitizer, she was ready for Michael's neat, tidy room. She was afraid to disturb anything, grimacing as she remembered getting raked over the coals at dinner once because she'd moved one of his knickknacks slightly after dusting. She wouldn't be sad to see him leave next year.

Placing the tangerine laundry bundle in the specific place Michael had designated for it on the southwest corner of his bed, Misty carefully backed out of his room into the hallway.

Stria's room was next. Misty wasn't quite sure how she felt about her yet. At first blush, Stria seemed extremely timid and shy, and she barely spoke at meals. Misty generally preferred people who were more open, but maybe Stria would open up in time.

That was one of the things that made Kaden so fun and easy to talk to. Most of the men who were chosen to work on the station were so much older than she was, and on those rare occasions when she got to meet somebody her own age, they were so full of themselves it was disgusting. Thankfully, Kaden wasn't like that.

Recalling herself to the task at hand, she moved on, angling past the refining room and the empty physician's quarters. *Too bad he decided to go back to Earth with the first set of scientists.* He'd realized too late that he wasn't cut out for life in space, and had snuck aboard the shuttle that was taking the first crop of scientists back home.

He hadn't told any of the station crew he was leaving, either—Jala only found out when she accompanied the scientists to the shuttle and found him there already, crouched inside. He refused to return with her and had insisted on going home. Jala told everyone what happened over dinner that day, though Misty could see that she wasn't happy about having to share the news.

Not having a doctor on staff had been terrifying at first—everyone was careful not to get even so much as a paper cut—but after a few months with no major injuries or illnesses, they were able to relax a little. Now she hardly ever thought about the fact that they didn't have a physician here. He hadn't been needed and hadn't been missed.

Stop daydreaming, girl, and get back to work, Misty chided herself, dropping off the clean laundry for her room next, then skipping along to Kirby's room, which was what she considered normal inside. Pictures of Kirby's family and friends adorned the walls and took up space on the counters.

Misty moved along to the next set of rooms—first Drake's, then Harris' and Jala's. Their rooms were all pretty similar—lived in, but not overly personalized. Jala, Misty knew, kept her most precious mementos in a locked box under the bed. Only a generic painting of an unknown cityscape and a worn photo of Jala's mother reminded you that she'd lived somewhere else before landing on Titan.

I know how Jala feels, Misty drifted off again. *Sometimes I forget I've ever lived anyplace else. It's been so nice to have a job where I matter, knowing that Jala and Harris and Ivy and Zevon are my friends. I'll be sad to return to Earth, lost in a sea of billions of other people, where I might as well be invisible. And even my own family—they'll be fourteen years older than they should be when I get home. I mean, even my little brother is older than I am now!*

She did some quick math in her head. She left at 18, while her brother was only 15. By the time she'd reached Titan, he was already 22, and she was still only 18. Now that she was 24, he was turning 28, and it would only be worse on the way home...everyone jumping ahead another seven years in time while she stayed the same age. *They're practically strangers as it is. It'd be so much easier if I could just stay here.*

Shaking her head wistfully, she pushed through the last of the laundry, walking past another angle in the building by the communications center, then depositing a bundle of royal blue laundry for Zevon and a lavender bundle for Ivy.

Misty and her automated laundry cart nearly strolled past the library, but something about the closed door didn't feel right. It was never closed during the day.

Curious, she pressed her hand to the door, regretting her decision the second it opened. Books had been tossed everywhere, and there, in the middle of the literary chaos, lay Dr. Kinney, dead.

Misty had never encountered a dead body before since everyone always went for cremation, and her mind was having trouble reconciling what she was seeing.

In a daze, Misty managed to activate her drones to sweep the dining room and hallways in preparation for dinner and after-dinner mingling.

She remained at the door, however, stuck in place. She couldn't stop staring at the dead body, horrified, while the busy drones hummed around her, cleaning as they went.

Several minutes later, Misty's mind came back from the far away place it had retreated to and told her what she was seeing. *Dr. Kinney is dead...dead...dead,* it screamed at her over and over again.

★★★★★★★★★

Kaden was the first one to make it back inside to the safety of the station, but once he got into the large bay, he realized that he needed to wait for Stria and Harris to return.

I really should have paid more attention to Jala's instructions about the airlock system yesterday, he thought miserably. *Now I'll have to wait who knows how long for Stria and Harris to get back. And I really don't want to give that man the satisfaction of relying on him for anything.*

Restless by nature, Kaden found himself pacing through the hangar, examining the other rovers to kill time. A little further back, almost like it was hugging the wall for protection, he came across a small ship. It had obviously been damaged by something, though he wasn't sure what. There was a dent in the nose of the craft as big as his head.

Nothing had corroded yet, but it had clearly been here for a few years by the thick layer of hydrocarbons coating the outside of the craft. It probably got blasted by a new layer every time the bay doors opened. All the seals appeared to be intact, though, and it didn't look like any Titanean grime had made its way inside the little shuttle.

Why are you here? he wondered. Jala hadn't mentioned it on their grand tour yesterday, but it didn't seem like it was being hidden from them. All you had to do was drive off in one of the surrounding rovers and it would be easily visible. He was still examining the shuttle when the unmistakable hum of a rover told him that Harris and Stria had finally made their way back to the station.

Smirking at the thought of having to show Kaden how to handle the airlocks for the second day in a row, Harris wondered yet again what these scientists would do without him and the Commander to take care of them. For his part, Kaden vowed to never be in this position again, and he paid careful attention this time as the Assistant Commander went through the whole procedure again for his benefit.

Stria looked like she was hearing this for the first time, too, so he didn't feel quite as foolish. Next time he'd remember—wait until the indicator light turns purple, THEN take off the helmets.

Going through the refining room process felt a little awkward with just the three of them; especially when two of them didn't exactly see eye to eye about things. Kaden was sure he caught Adley glaring at him out of the corner of his eye, though it could've just been the green goop making him squint.

"Miss Reese, if you'll allow me," Harris Adley said in his overly formal way, opening the door for Stria to enter the space station proper once they'd completed the cleansing process. Though he was just a step behind, Kaden saw the Assistant Commander intentionally back away from the door, causing it to nearly close on him as he was stepping through.

"Oops!" Harris grinned, turning to face the younger man. "I'll have to be more careful next time." He strode off with Stria while Kaden fumed silently, his face beet red.

I knew it! He is interested in Misty. Otherwise, he wouldn't have it out for me so bad. What an egomaniac. Well, two can play at this game, Assistant Commander!

Back in his room, Kaden carefully weighed his options behind the privacy of the locked door.

✯✯✯✯✯✯✯✯✯

"Harris, you really don't have to walk me back to my room," Stria said in exasperation. She felt that her bravery in the frigid Titanean air had earned her some degree of autonomy, and she didn't want to be treated like a little girl every time she turned around.

"I think you misunderstand, Miss Reese—Stria, I mean. I keep forgetting you don't go by formalities. Michael's room just happens to be in the same direction as yours, and after missing two meals in a row, I wanted to check in on him. So, you see, I have to go this way."

"Oh, sorry," she said meekly. "I kind of assumed you were babying me, after my behavior yesterday."

"I think you'll soon see that I don't **baby** anyone on this station. I have my orders to protect the civilian lives on this moon, and I take those orders very seriously. You don't understand the risks involved in…"

Stopping himself abruptly, he attempted to walk past Stria's door as though he hadn't said too much. As though he hadn't almost spilled a secret he promised Shan he'd take to his grave.

But Stria caught the momentary worry that flashed through his intensely brown eyes and wrinkled up his forehead—a look that seemed foreign on him.

"What risks don't I understand?" she demanded, wondering at the nerve of this man, assuming she couldn't handle whatever risks were associated with being out here. She'd already gone over every single one of them in minute detail in her mind, taking them apart, examining them and putting them back together. He didn't know a thing about her. Other than the fact that she was scared. That was it. Nothing about who she really was.

Harris scrutinized Stria's face, wisely waiting for the tempest to pass before he spoke again.

"I think you've assumed too much, Miss Reese. About me, for instance. Or about how things work on a space station. There are forces at play here that aren't well understood. How the mind handles stress in the depths of space hasn't been evaluated very well. I'm not trying to scare you; I just think you should be careful, that's all."

"I see—and are you going around warning everyone else to be careful? Or only me? Instead of dancing around the subject, why don't you admit that you don't think I can handle it up here? You and Ora are exactly alike, thinking that I'm only one moment away from running outside without the safety of a space suit! Did I get *that* assumption right?"

The force of her anger transformed Stria into something powerful, like the oceans she studied, waves of emotion filling the space between them.

The look on his face told her that was exactly what he did think about her. "You're nothing but a...a...pompous jerk!" she hissed, activating the automatic door and storming into the safety of her room.

She'd planned on saying something far worse, but her mouth wouldn't cooperate, and *jerk* was the most she could manage to choke out. *How dare he? Who does he think he is? Acting like some self-righteous superhero here to save us all from...what?*

And who said that just because I doubt myself sometimes, he gets to doubt me, too? I'm not going to have a nervous breakdown!

She threw her pillows in frustration and sank down onto the bed, head in hands, vowing not to waste one more thought on the man. She was still thinking about him, however, when the dinner chime sounded. The gentle concern in his eyes and the way his brown, close-cropped hair accentuated his good looks only crossed her mind a couple of times.

✫✫✫✫✫✫✫✫✫

It took Harris a few seconds to realize that Stria had done the equivalent of slam the door in his face—the smooth swish of the doors here didn't make much of an impact that way—and he wasn't sure how he felt about it. He couldn't help but wonder what it was about this woman that got to him so much.

He'd felt her superiority wash over him when they were out this afternoon, but he tried to brush it aside and not let it interfere with his mission, which was to keep civilians out of harm's way.

He'd worked with arrogant scientists before—why Reid, now, was one of the worst. But it didn't get under his skin the way Stria's attitude had. And her, pretending she wanted to do away with titles like Doctor that differentiated people, when she'd been thinking he was beneath her the whole time.

It wasn't titles, degrees, or education that divided people, it was that self-righteous attitude that crept in unnoticed when you were used to being around everybody who thought the same way you did. It was the hypocrisy that he hated.

In spite of all that, he could see a vulnerability in her that was (or could have been) appealing if she weren't trying so hard to pretend she wasn't afraid of everything out here. She hadn't fooled him for a minute. Or anyone else for that matter. Better to admit a weakness upfront and move on. No sense in trying to cover it up or pretend it wasn't there. That's when problems started.

*I'll never figure her out—better to not even try. After all, she's only one more scientist in a station full of them who will leave in a short time and be forgotten, like all the rest who came before her. I'll be damned if I waste one more thought on **Doctor** Reese.*

He was so preoccupied with not thinking about her that he forgot all about checking on Dr. Kinney, and was surprised to hear the dinner chime from inside his own room, unaware of how he'd gotten there.

8: The Body in the Library

Drake was in the middle of another argument with Kirby about the best way to clean the HVAC system when he realized Misty hadn't finished up her rounds.

He always kept a lookout for her lovely figure whenever he got the chance, and she usually passed the maintenance room twice during the day.

Today, however, he'd only seen her go by once. He made a quick excuse to Kirby about needing a coffee break, and since he'd last seen Misty heading that direction anyway, figured the dining room was a good place to look for her.

He'd only gone a few steps when he found her, standing silently at the library door, staring intently at something inside.

"Hey, what's so fascinating in there?" he grinned, putting an unwelcome arm around her shoulder.

She winced, pointed, and ran off down the corridor, finally

released from death's horrible spell.

It took Drake a while to realize what she'd been staring at—after all, he took his time gazing after her, enjoying the way her body moved as she ran. When she was finally out of sight, he turned back to the library, and suddenly understood where Mike had been all day.

Still not fully comprehending the scene before him, he ran in and tried to revive the fallen scientist, thinking he'd only suffered a concussion. After several minutes, Drake finally realized he was trying to save a dead man.

At least Mike didn't succumb to space sickness, Drake thought grimly, firmly closing the door and returning to the maintenance room to tell Kirby what happened.

"Are you kidding me?" she asked in disgust when he attempted to tell her what he'd seen. "I don't believe you! This isn't funny, you know!" She tossed her unruly blonde hair out of her face and glared at him so long, Drake backed away from her uncomfortably.

"I'm not lying—go see for yourself!" he finally shouted over the hum of the equipment surrounding them.

"I swear, if you're pulling some kind of stupid prank..." she began, stomping toward the library. She pounded against the door, and stopped short when she saw Michael crumpled among the books.

"See," Drake whispered in her ear, making Kirby jump.

"Why us? How come **we** always end up being the ones to find dead scientists?" Kirby was beginning to hyperventilate, and Drake quickly shut the library door until she calmed down and they had a plan of attack.

"Well," he said, engaging the lock, "what are we going to do about it?"

"Do? What do you think we're going to do? Tell Jala, of course, and leave the rest up to her."

"But this isn't space sickness—he just fell while trying to get a book—that's all."

Kirby whirled around on him, anger welling up inside. She knew it wasn't his fault, but she'd had just about all she could take of Drake's, well, Drakeness, and was looking for a reason to lash out.

"If you're so sure of that, then who closed the door?" she blustered, sure it was no accident.

"He did, of course, when he came in here. What's so strange about that?"

"Nothing, I guess. I don't know. This whole thing just seems...weird. I mean, the top shelf isn't even that high."

"Kirby, don't go looking for trouble when there isn't any. Mike fell while trying to get or put back a book, and that's all there is to it. He **was** getting older, you know. Maybe he had a heart attack or something."

She shot him a nasty look. "So now you have a medical degree? Are you a coroner all of a sudden?"

Drake was shocked at the venom in Kirby's voice. As if she wanted to kill **him**. He put out a cautious hand, trying to create a little distance between them.

"Kirby," he soothed, using the same calm voice as a lion tamer, "Mike fell and hit his head. That's all. There's nothing sinister going on here."

"We still have to tell Jala," she raged, wondering at the cruel twist of fate that tied her to Drake by not one, but two secretly dead bodies.

"Maybe we should just keep it to ourselves for now—that is, if you genuinely have concerns that it wasn't an accident."

"I never said that, Drake, and you know it. Stop twisting my words around."

"I'll leave it up to you—tell or don't tell. But whatever we do, we can't leave him here in the library."

"No, we can't, which is why we have to tell Jala. She'll know what to do," Kirby sighed, slumping a little under the weight of it all.

"I suppose we won't be allowed to tell anyone else about **this** body, either?" she quavered, passing a hand over her aching eyes.

"I'm sure it'll be okay to talk about this one—but we should probably let Jala know first, if you're sure you want to mention it to her."

"Of course I'm sure! We're telling her tonight at dinner."

"Fine, we'll tell her at dinner. Until then, let's make sure no one else opens this door on accident."

I'll just take care of Misty, Drake thought, *and make sure she doesn't fill the Commander's head with some nonsensical story first.*

9: Consultations

Dinner passed slowly for Ora, as she tried not to think about where Dr. Kinney might be. No one else seemed all that bothered by the fact that he hadn't been seen since last night, which made her feel even more alone and adrift than she already did.

The others all wanted to believe that he'd show up some time. She'd been fully hoping Michael was at the table already, waiting for her to sit down.

But when she got to the dining room, he was nowhere to be found. He wasn't there halfway through dinner, or when dessert was served, and he didn't show up before the others started heading off to play games or call it an early night.

It was as though no one wanted to acknowledge that anything was different—as if admitting that something could be wrong would make it true.

It was a philosophy Ora hated. It was always better to face the truth head-on, no matter how difficult.

✬✬✬✬✬✬✬✬✬

"So, how was guard duty today?" Jala quietly asked Harris over their steaming bowls of pho at dinner.

She'd thought it better to sit at the smaller table by themselves, and had gone so far as to remove the other chairs so no one would try to sit with them. Drake and Kirby had seemed stubbornly determined to catch her attention tonight, and she would not be pulled off-task.

Harris waited until there was enough noisy slurping from the other tables to mask his response. "She seemed fairly well composed, and while frightened, managed to complete her tasks well. I distracted her by having her drive us out to the lake."

He hoped his tone displayed disinterested duty, and not the sea of emotions she brought up in him.

"Good strategy. Well done, Harris. And there was nothing that concerned you as you watched her? Did she try to leave your sight, or act strange in any way?"

Harris tried to hide his grimace...she'd acted plenty strange to him, but he didn't think Jala wanted to hear how she'd managed to get under his skin. Instead, he offered woodenly, "Dr. Reese appeared to handle the conditions fairly well considering. She remained within my line of sight at all times."

Remembering the way she trembled slightly when they left the Mare, he added, "I still think it would be wise for one of us to accompany her for the first two or three weeks, and if she doesn't fall to pieces by then, it would probably be safe to allow her to be alone with the other scientists and no longer require our presence."

He was hoping Jala would take the hint and volunteer herself for this duty. After Stria's superior attitude today, and her defensiveness any time he tried to help her, he didn't think he'd be able to maintain his cool if he had to keep running her around the moon every day for the next two weeks.

"If you don't mind, then, Harris, I'd like to ask you to continue to accompany her." Catching his quick frown, she added, "I realize it's pulling you away from your real work, and I know you dislike babysitting as much as I do, but unfortunately, it can't be helped. I've had several urgent comms from NASA about the next shuttle and will be tied up for a while dealing with it."

Now this, at least, sounded interesting. "What's going on with the shuttle?" he pressed, almost knocking over the noodle bowl in his excitement.

Slowly twirling her noodles around a pair of chopsticks, Jala looked around the dining room carefully. Feeling reassured that the other tables weren't paying them the least bit of attention, she finally said in a low voice, "There's been some trouble tracking its whereabouts. Mission Control has been getting static when they attempt to decode the on-board navigation system's transmissions and can't confirm it's still on target for Titan next year. I'm working on triangulating their coordinates to see if, being closer, we can get a better idea of where they are. Maybe we'll be able to break through whatever's interfering with the comm systems."

Now it was Harris' turn to glance quickly around the room, sure that the news had been heard by someone else. No one was looking directly at their table, but...he whispered his reply to be on the safe side. "But that's never happened before, has it? To completely lose communication with a ship on its way here?"

"Not to my knowledge," Jala replied gravely, brows furrowed.

"There's some time to do course corrections if necessary—but we have to be able to communicate with the ship's navigation controls first. And so far, we haven't been able to do that. I can't hail the system. But don't you worry, Harris—I'll get them back on track, trust me. It goes without saying, of course, that we'll have to keep this between ourselves for now."

He nodded in agreement. Of course. This kind of news could make someone like Stria lose what little sense of stability she'd gained from today and run off into the smog-filled twilight in the middle of the night. The thought of Stria's pretty features twisted in frozen agony made him feel sick to his stomach. Pushing the bowl aside, he excused himself and rushed from the dining room.

✭✭✭✭✭✭✭✭✭

Misty was reluctant at first to join everyone else for dinner, but Drake had assured her that the best she could do for Dr. Kinney was to celebrate life.

He also urged her not to share the news with anyone else until he could talk to Jala, which made sense to Misty, though she was still struggling with what she'd seen.

At least she'd get to be with her friends at dinner, and while she couldn't talk about Michael's death, she could soak up their positivity and try to feel better.

After all, no matter what she did, Michael was still dead—there was no sense mourning a man she didn't even like.

She did her best to put on a happy face at dinner, and vowed that no one would know about her private problem until Jala chose to make the announcement herself.

✫✫✫✫✫✫✫✫✫

One of Zevon's favorite things about life on the station was that he and Ivy were treated like equals. Most of the people up here didn't seem to care about class, race, or position, but there were always one or two who somehow managed to sneak through the screening process in spite of everyone else's best efforts.

Reid Everly was one of those, unfortunately. Zevon did his best to avoid the self-righteous scientist at all costs.

Drake was another one. Zevon had his own special reasons for disliking the man: he'd tried repeatedly, and failed each time, to charm Ivy into his bed.

She had too much self-confidence and intelligence to be dazzled by Drake's playboy ways, which had only seemed to make him want her more. Zevon recalled the day she came to him on the verge of tears as she relived a particularly harrowing encounter with the would-be Romeo.

If Drake ever humiliates Ivy like that again, I'll make sure he regrets it, he thought, glaring at Drake's smug face across the dining room. *It's too bad we're all trapped here with him until end-of-mission.*

Making a concerted effort to pull his thoughts away from Drake,

Zevon worked hard to focus on the present, asking Kaden how his first full day on Titan had gone. A lot of the scientists were too serious to be much fun at dinner, but Kaden seemed a little more light-hearted than most.

"It was terrible!" he complained with a wink to Stria. He took a long swig of his tea, then immediately made a face. He'd forgotten for a moment that the beer-colored liquid wasn't really beer. It was a dry station, which Jala had explained in her best *this-is-for-your-own-good* tone when he'd asked what their options were at meals.

"For starters," he grinned at Zevon, "I nearly broke my back extracting cores from the frozen tundra out there while Stria here got to enjoy a quiet day at the beach. And to make matters worse, I missed Misty's pretty gray eyes all afternoon."

Turning to his right, he gazed deeply into said pretty gray eyes until she playfully slapped his arm and told him to stop making an ass of himself.

Thanks to Jala hijacking Adley almost the second he walked into the dining room, Kaden had encountered no resistance in his quest to spend time with the station's one-woman cleaning crew.

"Well played, Misty!" Zevon laughed. He liked this newbie.

Kaden exuded a zest for life, something that had been sorely lacking on the station for a long time. Ivy seemed to sense a difference, too—she was less reserved tonight than she'd been in months. Emboldened by Kaden's energy, he suggested, "Why don't we keep this going after dinner? Does everyone know how to play Pyramids?"

"That's my favorite!" Misty squealed, delighted that Zevon had suggested it. It would be the perfect way to take her mind off Michael.

"Kaden, I'll teach you," she offered quickly in a bright tone when he mentioned he'd never heard of the game.

Ivy happily agreed to join the game, and the two chefs made quick work of cleaning up the tables and setting out dessert, eager to get started on what promised to be a fun evening of Pyramids.

It was uncanny the change this young scientist had brought to the atmosphere. Stria, while nice enough, was too shy to contribute much, though she seemed eager to be part of the group, and Zevon didn't have high expectations that she'd leave much of a social footprint.

The truth was that Stria'd barely had a chance to talk during dinner. Unless someone was asking her a direct question (which was rare), she sat in frustrated silence as the others bantered back and forth easily. It was like she wasn't even there. She'd purposely sat next to Kaden tonight, hoping to catch Harris' eye when he came in for dinner. Not that she wanted Harris to be jealous or anything—she just wanted him to see that other people didn't seem to have issues with her.

But he made a beeline for the Commander's table and didn't even glance in her direction once. That humiliation was compounded by the fact that she'd been forced to listen to Kaden and Misty flirt through yet another meal. The few times Kaden faced her directly, she got tongue-tied from the pressure she put on herself to be witty and funny and make him laugh the way Misty did.

It was so frustrating, how easily some people could be the center of attention and have everyone hanging on their every word. She was tired of feeling like second fiddle to practically the whole world. Even up here, where she hoped things would be different with a much smaller group of people, it was the same old story. Not interesting enough on her own to draw people to her, or extroverted enough to mix easily, she hung back while everyone else got the guy, made new friends, and had fun without her.

Stria was desperate to get out of playing Pyramids tonight, even though she actually liked the hologram stacking game. But she wasn't about to spend the rest of her evening listening to Misty giggle coyly at every meaningless, flirtatious thing Kaden said to her, while Stria sat there in irritated silence.

In the middle of these less-than-happy, but very familiar thoughts, she saw Harris leap from his chair at the far end of the dining room like a scalded cat.

That's funny—I never would've imagined he could get so upset over anything, she mused. *He's usually all protocol and professionalism.*

Curiosity piqued, she decided to follow him out and made a quick excuse to her tablemates about having a headache and wanting to go lie down.

Now what? Needing some plausible reason for stalking Harris, and catching the dessert plates out of the corner of her eye, she grabbed the two closest to her on the way out of the dining room. It was a pretty weak excuse. She doubted he'd really believe she wanted to make sure he got dessert, but she felt it was better than showing up empty-handed.

Not that she wanted to spend any more time with Harris than was absolutely necessary—she was still mad at him, after all. But it must've been something serious to upset him so badly—and she was determined to show him that she could handle the hard truths of living up here no matter what. Besides, in a strange way, listening to other people's anxieties and troubles took her mind off her own and made her feel more confident.

She was grateful to get away from Misty. If Kaden weren't on the station, maybe they could've been friends. But now, the only thing Stria thought of when she looked at the younger woman was how unfair it was that Kaden had already fallen for her after only two days.

☆☆☆☆☆☆☆☆☆

Jala was a little hurt to see Harris rush off without even finishing dinner. They usually talked over dessert or joined a few of the others for whatever activities they'd come up with to amuse themselves. He had a soothing presence that seemed to be at odds with his tough military bearing, and of all the people on the station, Harris was the one she felt closest to. In fact, he understood her so well, he could almost read her mind.

As much as she loved feisty little Misty and her adventurous spirit (so much like a younger version of herself!) Harris would be the only person she really missed once their mission was over. She tried not to think about that...best to push it out of her mind.

End-of-mission would come someday, but thankfully not for a while yet. She still had a few years to enjoy her precious space station and revel in looking up at a sky that reminded her of peach cotton candy when the light hit the particulates the right way. And the majestic beauty of Saturn and her rings ruling over the sky—there was really nothing like it. Jala would've readily traded Earth's warmth and greenery for the views on this far-flung moon for the rest of her life, if NASA would've allowed it.

She felt guilty for making Harris responsible for Dr. Reese for the next few weeks. She could tell things hadn't gone well during their extended time together, but she had to focus all her energies on tracking down the errant shuttle and redirecting it.

Though it was just as much of a punishment on her to be without his company as it was for him to babysit a new scientist. There was no getting around it—they'd both have to be miserable for a few weeks, and then life could go back to normal.

✫✫✫✫✫✫✫✫✫

Seizing their chance, Drake and Kirby practically leapt at Commander Shan the second Harris left the dining room.

"We have to talk to you," Drake began, and seeing the look on Kirby's face, Jala relented, allowing them to join her.

10: Runners

Juggling the two plates of pecan pie proved to be harder than she thought—Stria was nearly running in order to catch up with the Assistant Commander's long, powerful strides.

Whatever had happened, he sure was in a hurry to escape being noticed, and in her haste not to lose him, she rounded the corner by the little library so fast that she nearly ran into her quarry and almost ended up wearing both of their desserts.

"Harris, hold on a second!" she panted, trying to catch her breath.

"I thought someone was following me," he rumbled quietly, hands on his hips, "but I'm surprised to see it's *you*..." The exertion brought out the color in her cheeks and complimented her delicate beauty. *Don't be a fool, Harris. Don't be a fool.*

"Sorry, I didn't mean to startle you," Stria said in a breathless half-apology.

"Have you been running?" he asked, with a little more urgency than normal, afraid of where she might have been off to in such a rush. Again, the unwanted image of her dead face flashed across his mind. "Is everything alright?" he pressed, looking deeply into her cornflower blue eyes.

"Funny, I was going to ask you the same thing," she said, recovering both her breath and her indignation at the same time. He was **not** going to treat her like a frightened little child.

"After the way you jumped up at dinner, I thought something must have upset you pretty badly, and I was coming to check on you."

"**You** were coming to check on **me**?" he asked incredulously.

Catching the curious glance he gave the dessert plates she was holding, Stria mumbled, "You left before they brought out dessert."

Looking around cautiously, Harris gently took her arm. Footsteps were approaching. *This won't do at all.*

"Why don't we talk about this someplace other than the hallway?" he said under his breath, guiding her so quickly to his room that she nearly fell along the way.

☆☆☆☆☆☆☆☆☆

Jala was a woman of action, and as soon as Kirby and Drake told her about Michael, she went to examine the scene for herself, questioning them the entire time about who else knew, what they thought had happened, and whether anyone else could've stumbled onto the body before they did.

Drake explained Misty was the one who (he believed) found Mike's body, and that he'd strongly warned her not to say anything.

Jala gave a curt nod of approval over the way he'd handled the situation. After a practical, but lengthy discussion, it was determined that Jala would inform everyone about Michael's unfortunate accident over breakfast the next morning.

In the meantime, she, Kirby, and Drake locked the body back up, and agreed to return around 2 a.m., when everyone else was sure to be in their rooms, to dispose of the body in the incinerator one floor below.

While it was harsh, there was no place to store a body on the space station, and they had no way of embalming him. It was best to get the unpleasant deed out of the way with as few witnesses as possible.

"Less chance of runners that way," Jala assured them, and Drake and Kirby agreed.

☆☆☆☆☆☆☆☆☆

"What was all the urgency about?" Stria asked once the door to Harris' room slid shut behind them, not sure whether to be angry that he'd practically dragged her down the hallway or gratified that he was going to take her into his confidence. She decided on a compromise of mild annoyance and expectation.

"I thought I heard footsteps...I couldn't risk anyone hearing something they shouldn't."

Seeing her glance at the door suspiciously, Harris rushed to reassure her.

"Don't worry—it'll be safe to talk in here. The doors are soundproofed as well as the walls," he continued, not sure where to go with the conversation next. Was he really prepared to tell someone else about the lost ship? Or the runners?

"Would you like some coffee?" he stalled, urging her to take a seat.

He wondered unhappily if he'd be able to keep any of his secrets from her. He couldn't understand why she affected him so much. It was probably a sign that he'd been in space too long. Again, he thought about how close end-of-mission was and welcomed the day he could return to Earth.

"That would be nice, thank you," Stria replied, jarring him out of his reverie. She hadn't been in anyone else's room yet, and took the opportunity while Harris was busy making their coffee to let her eyes soak up every detail of this unusual man's living space.

Everything was neat and orderly, much the way she assumed a military man's room would be. The walls were a crisp clean white, with pale spruce accents; she could almost smell the pine forest it evoked to her. It reminded her of home.

There didn't seem to be any personal touches on display at all. Not that it mattered—she wasn't here to study the man's history, she reminded herself crossly; she simply wanted some intel about life on Titan, even the terrifying aspects of that life. If she could plan for things ahead of time, they wouldn't be as scary if (or when) they actually happened.

As Harris bent down to hand her a steaming cup of coffee, the delicious pine scent grew stronger, and she realized it was actually his cologne. Pleasant, soothing, and strong.

*He **is** handsome in this light*, she thought distractedly, forgetting for a moment that he really wasn't her type. *It's only because I'm homesick, that's all.*

The last thing she wanted was to gratify Harris' ego by making him think she was interested in him. And she assumed he had a pretty big ego—he'd have to, to help run a space station and tell everyone else what to do all the time, wouldn't he?

"So," she said, stroking her hair anxiously with her free hand, "what's going on that's gotten you so upset you have to leave in the middle of dinner, and makes you too nervous to talk about it in public?"

She stared at him defiantly, practically daring him to say the wrong thing, while Harris frantically worked through how much he could or should tell her without making her want to run out into the perpetual twilight of Titan. Buying time, he took a slow sip of coffee, then thoughtfully chewed a piece of pie.

He finally decided that honesty was the best policy. It would be nice to share his burden with someone else; he only hoped that sharing it with Stria wasn't going to be a huge mistake.

"I'm not really sure how much to tell you," he faltered, "and I don't want to burden you with having to keep secrets from everyone else on the station...but..."

"Harris, I swear I can handle this—keeping me in the dark won't make me any less afraid, you know. At least if I know what to expect, I can be on my guard against it. I'm really not as helpless as you seem to think I am."

"I don't think you're helpless..." he said in exasperation, "just afraid, and trying to pretend you're not. That's what's dangerous—trying to ignore the fear or pretend it doesn't exist. I need to know I can trust you—that I can trust **anyone**—to handle what I'm about to tell them without losing their heads. Can I rely on you, Stria?" He peered at her searchingly.

She didn't rush into speech, which Harris respected. It looked like she was actually taking her time to weigh her options.

When she finally spoke, it was with an air of finality. "Yes, you can trust me. I might not like what you have to tell me, but I'll let you know if I start to feel overwhelmed—deal?"

She smiled nervously, possibly her first non-judgmental gesture toward the Assistant Commander since she'd landed here.

"Deal," he said, relieved at what seemed to be a promising first step, noticing that she'd finally stopped stroking her hair. Maybe she would be okay, after all. He took a deep breath and plunged bravely—or foolishly—ahead.

"According to NASA, the shuttle that's on its way here has disappeared from all tracking systems. We don't know if it's still on course for Titan or if something happened during the flight to alter its trajectory. We can't even be sure anyone on board is still alive. If the communication system has failed, there's a high probability other systems on the ship have failed as well. Jala didn't say so, but I think she's worried that the next group of scientists might not make it here alive."

This was exactly the kind of thing Stria had been afraid would happen to **her** ship.

"What about radar? I know that's not really the right term for space, but can't we ping it somehow and determine if it's on the proper course?"

"Jala didn't share much, but I gather that she can't even do that."

Stria saw the concern on his face, but it was several degrees lighter than the look he'd worn when he rushed from dinner. Something darker was weighing on him. But what?

"Ok, I agree that doesn't sound good—but it also doesn't seem like something that would make a seasoned Assistant Commander, who I'm guessing would have to be used to hearing bad news by now—run from the dining room," she surmised.

"What else is going on?"

The startled look on his face told her she was right.

"How did you know—I mean, why should there be anything else? Isn't this bad enough? People will die if we can't bring them safely into Titan's atmosphere."

"You don't think I can handle what's really going on here," Stria accused. In spite of herself, her face turned deep crimson, the way it always did when she felt any strong emotion. She hadn't wanted Harris to see that he could get to her. And now he had.

"No, that's not it...I was thinking of something else, it's true. I'm not sure that I'm ready to share it with anyone. It's not because of you."

He seemed displeased that he'd upset her, which was curious—he sure hadn't seemed to mind earlier today. Stria wasn't sure how to take his present attitude, and wisely decided to finish her pie instead of saying the first thing that popped into her head.

Seeing that the lovely woman before him *(God help me, she is beautiful!)* wasn't bolting out the door or hurling insults at him gave Harris the push he needed to go on.

"I haven't discussed this with anyone else except Jala...so please keep that in mind. I haven't had much practice in talking about it..."

She cocked an interested eyebrow, and Harris continued, slowly letting the air out of his cheeks as he began.

"We've had a couple of, well, what we call 'runners' on the station during its operation. I don't know how much you know about space sickness?"

"They warned us about it in training, of course," Stria said around a mouthful of pie, hoping this wasn't going to lead back to her and her insecurities.

"Well, it seems that it affects people in different ways, and to varying degrees. I'd only ever heard of it making people listless, disinterested, or causing them to become irrationally angry."

"Yes, go on..." Stria tried to sound encouraging but wasn't sure if she succeeded. *This had better not be coming back around to me,* she thought nervously.

"Well, what we discovered was...it seems that...I'm sorry—I'm floundering a little." He took a deep steadying breath.

"The first group of scientists who came here in 2095 also had a medical doctor and a psychologist on board. They were supposed to stay with the crew until end-of-mission in 2104. They were studying the effects of Titan's unique atmosphere on the body and mind, making sure the rest of us held it together." *Oh God, the irony of **that***.

He paused and rubbed his temples. When he continued, his voice was softer.

"Anyway, the physician didn't make it that long. A couple years ago, Kirby and Drake found his body right outside the emergency doors. They'd been doing some work on the air ducts outside the station and were walking their way around the hexagon, checking vents as they went along. They got to the emergency airlock and found Dr. Kamura lying just outside the airlock door, dead.

"The only thing we could think of was that he'd decided to go exploring and gotten lost in the fog. He must've panicked, because his suit was torn in several places, which proved fatal when the damaged suit let in Titan's toxic frozen atmosphere. The worst part was that he'd almost made it back to the station; his body was only a few feet away from the door.

"Jala believed she'd failed him in some way. I tried to tell her there was nothing she could've done, but it deeply affected her."

Stria sat in rapt attention; she'd never heard of anything like this happening before. They certainly hadn't told her during training that suicide was one of the symptoms of space sickness.

"But what makes you think it **was** space sickness?" she probed, the words echoing her thoughts. "That could have been caused by anything, right? I mean, he took the time to put on a suit and make sure he was protected from the elements. Granted, if he got disoriented, I can see how he'd maybe start to be afraid, but to the point he was tearing at his suit, killing himself?"

"Commander Shan thought Dr. Kamura had gotten confused, forgetting he was on Titan and not Earth, and felt like he needed to take a stroll—but his survival instinct kicked in temporarily and he at least put on the space suit. She didn't think it was intentional—that our physician wanted to harm himself in any way—but rather that being here had affected his mind to the point that he couldn't separate reality from fiction. We have no way of knowing what he thought he was doing when he began gashing his suit like he did."

Stria could hear the genuine sorrow in his voice. *Ok, so he cares about the people who come here; he's not totally robotic and duty-bound.*

"Please go on," she urged gently, sensing there was more to come.

"Sometimes it does happen that people miss Earth so much they imagine they're still there—talking to imaginary friends, seeing Earth's moon over every alien horizon. That inability to reconcile being in space becomes too much for them and they suffer a break from reality. Dr. Thompson, our staff psychologist, explained that sometimes space sickness does work that way. We'd never seen anyone harm themselves, though. But it seems we still have a lot to learn about how space sickness affects people—and the types of people likely to succumb to it."

Stria imagined what it would have been like to find a body. She shivered in spite of the warm room.

"How did Kirby and Drake handle finding Dr. Kamura's body?"

"They took it pretty well considering," Harris said with a slight grimace. "Jala told them that it must have been a terrible accident. We thought that would be the end of things, and we'd never find another runner."

"Runner?"

"That's what we call people who get this form of space sickness— runners—because it seems like they're running away from something, or running toward something."

"But doesn't everyone know what happened to the physician? I mean, he's obviously not here anymore—and surely Kirby and Drake told someone about him—right?" Stria took a sip of her now cool coffee, trying to take everything in.

"No...well, I mean, it's kind of complicated. Jala was afraid that if the others found out what happened, they'd panic—and we'd have a whole station full of runners. So she made up a story that he left when the first group of scientists went home—right before Reid and Michael got here. She said he'd decided he wasn't cut out for life in space and wanted nothing more than to go home. Nobody ever questioned her on it; why would they? Jala incinerated his remains, and she swore Kirby and Drake to secrecy. We didn't think it was wise to tell anyone else because we didn't want to put ideas in people's heads."

Harris looked expectantly into his coffee cup, as if it could tell him what to say next. Stria, noting his hesitation, took advantage of the momentary silence to ask another question.

"If I'm understanding all this correctly, you think Dr. Kamura, who was supposed to be field-tested and approved for a long-term stay on Titan, cracked under the strain of living in space after only three years and became the first known death from space sickness? I don't mean to sound sarcastic; I'm just struggling to understand it all. I mean, sitting here in your room, with a cozy fire going after a gourmet meal and dessert, it seems impossible that someone, no matter how much they missed Earth, could snap like that."

Don't let on how close you came to doing the same thing when your own shuttle landed, Stria. Keep it together. Harris needs to believe I'm still trustworthy.

He looked intently at his companion, wondering if he'd said too much. He wondered, too, if he'd have to set up watch outside her room tonight, just to be on the safe side.

"I'll admit, it does seem a little far-fetched. I didn't want to believe it myself at first, either. And I guess I really didn't, until it happened again."

Why did I say that? I'm probably pushing her over the edge right now…I never should have said anything at all. He probed her eyes deeply, looking for any signs of panic.

"What?! Someone else decided to take a pleasant stroll in poisonous air in 300 degree-below-zero weather?" She stared hard at his shadow-shrouded features to be sure he wasn't teasing her.

"Dr. Reese, are you okay that I'm telling you all this? Maybe I shouldn't be, you know. You're not feeling…overwhelmed…are you?"

Stria wanted to be insulted but the obvious care written over his features made her hesitate. He wasn't trying to hurt her, he just wanted to be sure she was okay. She couldn't fault the guy for that. And she really did feel fine—so far.

"It's alright—you can go on. My scientific curiosity's been piqued and I'd like to hear more—if you think you can handle re-telling it."

She'd noticed for the first time that his hands were trembling from reliving the recent past. She moved beside him and took his hands in hers to stop them shaking (clearly, that was the only reason). She felt a little bit stronger thinking she was helping him in some way.

"You really don't have to do that," Harris spluttered, eyes wide, embarrassed that she was comforting him, when he'd convinced himself that she was the fragile one on this station. Well, maybe they'd both made some incorrect assumptions about each other. And, he had to confess, it felt good to be touched again after all these years. The last woman who'd held his hands like this was his former fiancée. And then he felt guilty for thinking of Stria that way.

He reminded himself that she was his charge, just like all the other civilians on this base, not some woman he was trying to pick up. Gently, so as not to hurt Stria's feelings, and more reluctantly that he wanted to admit, he extricated his hands from hers, making a pretext of needing more coffee.

After both their cups were full once again, Stria prodded Harris to continue.

"So you were saying that you found someone else who…followed in the good doctor's footsteps?"

"Yes, it's funny—only a few weeks later, Dr. Thompson himself...but this time, it was Jala and I who found him. The strange thing is, he wasn't wearing a suit. No helmet, no breathing apparatus of any kind—nothing to protect himself from the cold. He must have been freeze-dried almost instantly. How he even made it outside the bay doors in the first place is a mystery."

Harris fidgeted a little, realizing he'd said far more than he'd intended, but the understanding look on Stria's face led him to continue recklessly on.

"He should've been frozen solid from the initial blast of Titan's subzero atmosphere when the doors opened. I would've expected him to have dropped to the floor inside the bay, but he was completely outside the station and the doors were closed tight. I couldn't understand it—I still can't. Even worse than seeing his agonized face was the fact that his arms were stretched out, like he was reaching for something...or desperately trying to reopen the doors."

"How can you be so sure he fell victim to the same thing Dr. Kamura did?"

"You had to know Dr. Thompson. In his three years on the station, he'd never once expressed a desire to go out alone. And he rarely volunteered to leave with anyone else, for that matter. He had no interest in the external world we're on—he only wanted to explore what he called the 'inner world' of the mind. He made all of us come see him on a weekly basis and took copious notes about everything we said during each session. Watching, I think, for any signs we might decide to go wandering ourselves. So, you see, it wouldn't have made any sense—if he'd been in his right mind—for him to leave the station by himself."

Stria sat in fascinated silence as Harris continued. He was relieved to see that she did, in fact, seem to be holding herself together fairly well.

"When Dr. Thompson died," he went on, "Jala was devastated that she wasn't able to see the signs in time to prevent his death—and she was determined it would never happen again. We've been holding steady for the past two years, and we keep a much more vigilant eye on everyone now than we used to."

Seeing Stria's doubtful look, Harris added guiltily, "I've debated whether we should tell the others or not. It's been incredibly difficult to keep something so massive from them. I think, however, seeing as no one else has managed to go for a lone walk after bedtime, we made the right decision. Jala's theory is that Dr. Thompson knew about the physician's worsening mental state because of our mandatory weekly sessions and that's what eventually led him to do the same thing."

"If everyone else believes Dr. Kamura abandoned his post to go back home, which seems so unkind, by the way, then what did you say about Dr. Thompson? There wasn't a conveniently timed shuttle heading back home at that moment—was there?"

Harris was beginning to feel a little nauseous now that he'd been confronted with the magnitude of the lies they'd told, and how it sounded to an outsider. Maybe they'd been wrong, after all. It certainly sounded worse to him now that he was having to recount it all to Stria. He closed his eyes and tried to put the most positive spin on the whole thing that he could.

"Jala told everyone that Dr. Thompson was taking measurements of chemicals in the atmosphere to study their effects on the brain and accidentally fell into one of the Mares. No one would think twice about there not being a body. She couldn't risk herself to fish someone out of the freezing Mare and a body would sink so deeply it would never be seen again. It was a good story...."

Harris trailed off with a slight shrug of his shoulders.

"That's what we told each other, anyway."

"And the Mares are large enough that it would take decades to map them entirely. So if I'd heard the story and didn't find a body, I wouldn't question it, because it could have been in a different part of the lake. Did you really dump his body in one of the Mares?"

"No...that was just the cover story. He was incinerated, like Dr. Kamura. Taking him to one of the Mares would've been too much of a risk, since we'd have to use one of the rovers to get there. If anyone saw three people go out, but only two come back, it would've raised questions."

"I see," murmured Stria, carefully reviewing this new data. "And you've been keeping your secret for years now...yes, I see," she repeated, wondering how much the strain of this hidden knowledge affected Shan's manner toward the others.

Harris looked at her with tired, pleading eyes. His expression was begging her to understand the need to keep this between themselves. Something else was there, too. *Guilt*, she realized with a flash.

It was an odd juxtaposition for a tough military man. Stria felt almost compelled to kneel down next to him, take his hands in hers, and tell him that everything was going to be alright. The very thought made the heat rush to her face and she forced it as far away as possible.

"You look like you could use some rest," she finally said instead. "I should go. Don't worry—your secret's safe with me."

She gave his shoulder a quick, reassuring squeeze and then fled to her room before the dangerous image of herself at his feet could reassert itself. The last thing she needed was to get any more tangled up with the Assistant Commander than she already was.

It had been a mistake to get this close to him, letting her guard down like that, and acting as his confidante. She didn't like to admit how good it felt to have his full attention, to be alone with him, sharing coffee, sharing secrets. She was more drawn to him than she ought to be. He wasn't her type at all. Was he?

This will never do. Stop it, now, Stria—stop it!

She'd almost made it back to her room unseen. Certainly, she hadn't been aware of anyone else.

Commander Shan was making her usual midnight rounds, ensuring that everyone was in their rooms. She'd never seen anyone on her nightly watch until now. *What is Stria doing in Harris' room? And at this hour?* She checked her chronometer to make sure—yes, one a.m. Earth time. Jala didn't like the look of it; she didn't like it at all.

11: Secret Plans

D rake was always very careful not to be seen by Shan on her nightly trek around the station. He couldn't have her putting an end to his late-night fun. *Fun, oh God, what a joke that was,* he thought ruefully.

Tonight, he ducked behind one of the gigantic potted ferns as soon as he heard her footsteps; their thick, jade fingers gave him the advantage of seeing without being seen. It was only after he heard her door glide shut that he tiptoed from his hiding place and silently crept back to his own room.

Out of the corner of his eye, he glimpsed Stria tiptoeing from Harris' room. *Why, the old hypocrite!* Drake thought salaciously. *Telling everyone else to keep their hands off while he goes in for the kill.*

He didn't really mind; how the others wanted to fill their nights was up to them. All he cared about was avoiding Shan's watchful gaze. He'd always been successful up to this point—at least, he assumed he'd been, as she'd never spoken to him about it. And this was exactly the kind of thing she'd be sure to mention.

Although he thought of her as a friend, his only one on the station, he knew she wouldn't approve of his late-night hobby.

Trying to fix up the damaged shuttle in the bay had begun as a fun little project. It was a good way to burn off steam when things got too hard to handle up here, and had helped him stay sane far longer than he thought he'd be able to.

But he knew how Jala would react if she found out—giving him a motherly lecture about how dangerous it would be to even try and repair the craft, let alone use it for spaceflight. And then out of an abundance of caution, the space shuttle would be dismantled so nobody else would get any bright ideas.

Or maybe Shan's lapdog Harris would rigidly enforce his curfew— out of duty and to "protect the civilians" of course. As if, being an engineer, Drake didn't know his way around all the electronic components on that shuttle anyway. He wasn't about to accidentally blow anyone up in their sleep! But Harris didn't have the imagination to understand that.

Technically, there was nothing that said he couldn't work on repairing the shuttle. But after he and Kirby discovered Dr. Kamura's body, it had begun to feel less like a hobby and more like a necessity.

Not that he didn't trust his fellow crewmates with his secret, but being cooped up in a sealed space station did strange things to people sometimes. And he was starting to worry that someone else might try to steal his ship out from under him in a half-baked attempt to leave the station, especially once the news of Mike's "accident" got out.

Now why am I being so suspicious? He marveled at himself. *There's no reason to think anything sinister's going on, just like I told Kirby.*

Still, the suspicion lingered. Drake could feel himself slipping sometimes, and worried this new cynical mindset was another indication he needed to leave Titan and return to the sanity of Earth.

Getting the shuttle space-worthy was no longer just a way to pass the time, it was now his lifeline to Earth; a chance at escape, and he didn't want anything to jeopardize that.

So, it remained Drake's little secret. And he was doing a fabulous job of keeping it, he congratulated himself, as he slid into his room, secure in the knowledge that Jala had already turned in for the night.

He was only a few days away from making it flight worthy. If all went well, a week after he'd fully repaired the shuttle, he would sneak into the bay with his travel bags (after Shan's nightly rounds were finished, of course) and make his escape. He wasn't going to stick around for four more years and let his mind slowly fall apart.

Even though it was one of the smaller shuttles, there was still room for six passengers on the return flight. He ran through the list of possible travelers, hoping he'd be able to convince Kirby to join him.

✫✫✫✫✫✫✫✫✫

Kaden was in the mood for a late-night snack. On his way to the dining room, he spotted Drake hiding behind one of the giant potted ferns. *What the hell? Does Drake think he's in some kind of spy movie?*

Feeling self-conscious, Kaden imitated Drake and hid behind one of the gigantic potted plants himself. He patiently watched as the other man made his cautious way to the hangar with a bag of something or other slung haphazardly over his shoulder.

What is that man up to? Kaden wondered, bewildered. Shaking his head, he walked back to his own room deep in thought, snacks forgotten.

12: Revelations

Stria's alarm woke her much too early. She regretted listening to the Assistant Commander's stories last night, and she could already tell today was going to be rough.

Her eyes refused to stay open, and it took her twice as long to get herself dressed. Unfortunately, she had a full day planned at the lake, trying to map it out as far as possible with Harris' help. They'd only gone about thirty feet from shore in their test run yesterday, and she hoped to extend that to about 120 feet today if they could manage it.

She was both afraid to encounter whatever they'd seen yesterday and hopeful they would. She wanted it to be more than a fluke, but she didn't want to find anything that could actually harm her.

Stria was grateful to find that Kaden was the only one at breakfast when she came in. She wasn't sure she was ready to see Harris Adley again so soon, before she'd even had her coffee for the day.

Breakfast among the scientists was fairly subdued for various reasons. Kaden, because he'd spent a late, but awesome, evening playing pyramids with Misty. Zevon and Ivy had been there, too, of course, but he'd barely noticed them—and he was pretty sure that Zevon was completely taken with Ivy, too. *No competition to worry about there,* Kaden thought happily.

He was disappointed not to see the object of his affection at breakfast this morning, but maybe the crew ate their meals on a different schedule than everyone else.

Ora walked in briskly right after Stria had slowly shuffled to Kaden's table. Though she'd also been up late, going over and over all the implications of fossil life on Titan, she felt energetic and full of life this morning.

Even if nothing greater than microscopic mollusks were ever discovered here, it would still change everything humanity knew about life. She'd spent hours trying to frame her communications with Earth in exactly the right way since they'd have to be filtered through Shan and Adley. Even now, she was rehearsing how to phrase these revelations in a way that Shan couldn't garble.

✫✫✫✫✫✫✫✫✫

Reid had been studying some fascinating bacteriological samples, brought helpfully in by Dr. Reese yesterday, and his thoughts were consumed by life of the microscopic variety—taking very little notice of the human life all around him this morning.

Instead, he fidgeted distractedly with his plate, almost resentful of the fact that he had to eat and spend precious time away from his studies. But if he could crack the code to the microbes' ability to convert deadly combinations of hydrocarbons, cyanides, and carbon dioxides into life-giving fuel, it could change everything.

Think of it! All that fossil fuel pollution on Earth could be converted into something that could give life to a new type of organism, and just maybe reverse the course of global warming.

He, Reid Everly, could have the key to single-handedly saving his home planet. Wouldn't that be something? No more working and living in the shadows for him—no more being someone else's assistant! Throngs of people would flock to him to hear how he'd figured it all out.

He'd be pursued from one end of the planet to the other! It would be sweet revenge. The people who once thought of him as nothing but a helper, a lab rat, throwing themselves at his feet as the new savior of the human race. He could just picture it now...

Commander Shan arrived with an air of importance, breaking into his beautiful daydream to make an announcement. She commed the crew, then waited until everyone was seated, including Ivy and Zevon, before reciting the terrible events of the day before. She concluded by saying that the best way to honor Michael's memory would be to carry on with the day's tasks.

Ora no longer had to wonder what had become of her colleague—apparently, he'd fallen in the library sometime after she left and broken his neck or given himself a killer concussion, no one was exactly sure which.

She felt terrible. If only she'd waited around a little longer, she could've helped him find whatever he'd been looking for.

She glanced around the room, and noticed that several faces were turned suspiciously toward Reid. It was true that he had no love for Dr. Kinney...but this was an accident. Wasn't it?

Stria, for her part, couldn't believe how cold Commander Shan was about the whole thing, and was suddenly eager to get outside the station today and away from this insanity. She was horrified to think she and Harris had actually been right outside the library while Michael was in there, dead or dying.

What an awful way to die, and what an awful way to be 'honored'! she thought, abruptly leaving the dining room in disgust.

Shan commed Harris to retrieve Stria and ensure she completed her tasks for the day—she had a feeling this news would be especially rough on the fragile young woman.

Although it was necessary, Jala was beginning to regret insisting that Harris accompany Stria on her outings. But since she was stuck in the command center trying to contact the rogue shuttle, she didn't really have any other choice. After watching Stria leave his room so late last night, however, and not getting a satisfactory reply about why, Jala wondered if leaving them alone together for long periods of time might be a mistake.

Harris had reassured her there was no cause for alarm; he knew how she felt about the permanent crew getting too close to the visiting scientists.

☆☆☆☆☆☆☆☆☆

In spite of the terrible news about Dr. Kinney, Kaden was in a good mood. After all, why should he feel sad about the accidental death of a man he barely knew?

He was getting to work inside the station today, and being indoors meant he'd have a much better shot at spending time with Misty. Without wasting a second thought on whether it was appropriate under the circumstances or not, Kaden whistled a happy tune as he entered what had been designated as the geology lab.

To his dismay, it shared a clear glass wall with Reid's lab, so it was almost like he'd be working with the creepy man all day.

He hoped sound didn't carry between the walls—the last thing he wanted was to listen to Reid talk about more incredibly detailed, and incredibly boring, discoveries he'd made here. Or worse, to have to listen again to how important Reid thought he was. To hear him talk, the station would be lost without him.

Kaden felt slightly guilty for disliking the man so much—but knowing that most of the station felt the same way he did made it easier to pile on the reasons why Reid was so awful. Not that Kaden was going to go out of his way to be mean or anything, but he might have to start avoiding the man. And getting down to work would be the best way, at present, to do just that.

Besides, even though his first task for the day—analyzing the samples he took yesterday—was fairly routine and mundane, he was looking forward to seeing what chemicals the "soil" of Titan contained. It was hard to get it through his head that it was solid ice, not rock, though it was dense enough to be as tough as any rock back on Earth.

Kaden carefully used the finest setting on his cutting laser to slice small cross-sections from one of the cores he'd pulled up yesterday. Although he felt like a fool for doing it, he was wearing a station-issued breathing apparatus, specially insulated silicone gloves, and an outer garment that reminded him of the footy pajamas he used to wear as a little kid.

Supposedly those things would keep him protected from any alien bacteria that had hitched a ride into the station with his samples. He'd also had to place each sample inside a supercooled clear silicone rectangle to maintain a consistent subzero temperature, and to prevent alien bacteria from escaping into the lab and contaminating the station.

Of course, he was grateful for the precautions, but it was frustrating to have to work through so many layers of protection.

He opted to check out some of the more colorful core sections in the sample first, and carefully analyzed a rusty section with the spectrometer. While that was working on a chemical composition for him, he ran another similarly colored slice through a remotely operated electron microscope to see what he could, well, see.

Minute sworls in the ice core caught his eye. They almost looked like tiny little shells of some kind, but he knew it was his imagination creating a familiar shape out of something he'd never seen before.

After all, everyone knew there was no life on Titan—in the past or the present. He was trying his best to draw what he was seeing in his notebook (and doing a terrible job of it), when the spectrometer dinged at him, letting him know the chemical analysis of the other sample was ready.

Kaden thought he was seeing things at first. *The machine must have malfunctioned,* he told himself.

He checked the results twice and placed another sliced sample from the same core section into the machine to retest it, getting the same results. Checking the machine over thoroughly, Kaden had to finally admit that it seemed like everything was in good working order.

But it didn't make any sense for there to be oxygen in the sample. This section had come from seven hundred feet below the moon's surface, so the segment of time he was looking at would've been tens of thousands of years old. No one had ever guessed that there was free oxygen in the Titanean atmosphere once upon a time.

And just look at the helium and hydrogen signatures from the same era! He couldn't believe he was thinking this, but it looked a little bit like the atmospheric signature of a pre-contaminated Earth.

✫✫✫✫✫✫✫✫✫

Ora automatically bent her steps to the lab, though her mind was preoccupied with Michael's mysterious death, as she was beginning to think of it.

*What if Reid **did** do something to get Dr. Kinney out of his way? He obviously hated the man.*

She tried her best to brush away these uncomfortable suspicions by examining a tan 2-foot by 4-foot sample with many blobs, blots, and blotches.

It had been the specimen Michael was most excited for her to look at, and as such, seemed like a fitting project for today.

Every so often, she couldn't help risking a glance through the lab walls to Reid, who was just as absorbed in his work as ever. *I wonder if he ever thinks about anyone but himself,* she thought unkindly.

Returning to her own work, she magnified the blobs and blotches until stunning images took shape. They were much larger versions of the miniature mollusks she'd examined yesterday. Several, in fact, were visible with the naked eye, the largest being nearly three inches long. It was one of the most beautiful things she'd ever seen.

She reviewed Dr. Kinney's notes on the chunk before her, and discovered it was unearthed when the Station was under construction by the work crews, who thought it might be worth hanging onto.

A million questions flooded Ora's logical mind. *How could these creatures breathe without oxygen? Or grow large enough to be seen without a microscope? And what did they use for food?*

She squinted at one creature in particular. This one was shaped like an ancient eel. It appeared that there were three swimming nodes—one on each side and one on the creature's belly, unless that was its back.

Maybe these nodes helped to stabilize the animal in the thick seas of a subzero methane-ethane mixture. *But was it subzero then? And would it still have been a liquid petroleum sea?*

She flipped the slab over to see the name Charley handwritten on the back. Dr. Kinney must have named the creature.

Suddenly Ora wished she'd gotten a chance to know the man better, and vowed to herself to determine what really happened. Though of course it would be next to impossible without his body.

If only Shan hadn't incinerated it, she thought helplessly.

The overwhelming futility of it all threatened to spill from her eyes, so she forced her mind back to the specimens in front of her instead of the mysterious death she'd probably never get to the bottom of.

Could Titan have been a proto-Earth? she posed to herself. *What if it was closer to the Sun once upon a time, filled with liquid water and blue skies? What happened to change the atmosphere so much?*

Slowly, it began to dawn on Ora that this was the work of a lifetime. Not that microscopic mollusks were anything to sneeze at, but discovering life forms that developed parallel to those on Earth? That was the path to scientific immortality!

She let her eyes lovingly caress every last inch of the mysterious world that was hidden away in this miraculous ice slab, and began the impossible task of unraveling the frozen mysteries of prehistoric life on Titan.

13: Too Many Bodies

Stria was steeling herself for a full day with Harris. Her one cup of coffee at breakfast hadn't been nearly enough, and she was still reeling from the news about Michael's death.

While it was shocking, dwelling on it wouldn't do her any good. She felt her best bet was to pretend like his death had never happened. After all, what good would come from thinking about it?

She found herself grateful for the bulky spacesuits more than once on the journey back to the frigid lake. It created a safe distance between herself and Harris, and the helmet made it harder to read facial expressions. The last thing she wanted was to talk about Michael, or rehash what they'd discussed last night.

She didn't want to give Harris the wrong impression—though at this point, she wasn't sure which would be the wrong impression: that she was interested in him, or that she wasn't.

Harris, for his part, didn't seem very talkative today, and he'd had her drive to the Mare again. Wherever his thoughts were taking him, he wasn't sharing them with her. Which was fine, of course. He didn't owe her anything. And she didn't owe him anything either, for that matter. Really, all she promised to do was keep his secret, and that wasn't as much for him as for everyone else on the station.

But truth be told, it was a little frustrating to be so completely in his confidence last night and then be left in the dark today. *Does he know anything about Michael's death? What else is he hiding from me?*

Stria shook her head violently to clear her thoughts. Time to get back to why she was here—studying the Titanean seas for any signs of life.

When they got to Kraken Mare, she practically leapt out of the rover and began unpacking the probe with furious activity. Thankfully, Harris seemed too absorbed in whatever he was thinking to notice.

He hadn't slept well after Stria'd basically run away from him, tossing and turning most of the night, afraid he'd said too much. He wasn't sure she was stable enough to handle that kind of information. He wasn't even sure about his own stability most days.

What if her fears eat away at her until she, too, becomes a runner? His nightmare vision of her twisted, frozen face was becoming more and more real. *I never should've asked her to drive today,* he thought glumly. It meant he had nothing to think about but their time together last night. And her lovely, compassionate face.

Only time would tell if he'd been wrong to share his secrets with her. He was especially anxious to see how today went, and was very careful to remain within five feet of her at all times, just in case.

Michael's death barely broke through the surface of his thoughts. It had been natural, not a runner incident, so he didn't give it much importance. Besides, he was only temporary, and Harris didn't form emotional attachments to the visiting scientists.

Until now. He glanced quickly at Stria. She seemed to be doing ok so far, just a little too excited about getting the probe up and running. She hadn't been very talkative today, but neither had he. His hands fumbled a little with the Terratent when he remembered the way she'd touched him last night, and the look she gave him before leaving.

I can't let myself get caught up in these childish daydreams. She obviously didn't mean anything. And we hardly know each other! She's only temporary, he sternly reminded himself.

If Jala knew what he was thinking, she'd be furious. There had always been a firm no-relationships-with-the-temps policy, and he was dangerously close to breaking that rule. How stupid of him. Whatever closeness they'd felt last night was probably just from the intimacy of sharing a secret, nothing more than that.

Don't read more into this than there really is, he cautioned himself. Sighing inwardly, he realized that this was going to be a very long day.

"Ok, I think I've got it all set up. If you could do a quick double-check before I get the probe into the methane, I'd appreciate it," Stria said curtly, trying not to betray emotion of any kind.

Harris stiffly gave her the all-clear for the equipment, and the probe was off and running. Time to see if there was anything special going on today. He moved closer to Stria for her own protection, of course. *No other reason, just looking out for the civilian,* Harris lied to himself.

The probe's light searched the gloomy depths of the Mare, foot by pitch-black foot. Stria thought there was movement at the edges of the camera's view from time to time, but for the first hour, nothing obvious appeared. She was beginning to think it would be a boring day of staring at nothing but black screens when she saw it again—the same shape as yesterday. She tapped Harris on the arm to be sure he was paying attention.

"I see it," he said, mesmerized by the slow undulating movements of the bright creature captured on the lens. Moving more slowly today, they could see it was no eel—at least, no Earthly eel.

While sharing a similar shape, it was wider and flatter—like an eel that got steamrolled. And it didn't seem to have eyes, but maybe in the thick darkness of the Mare, it didn't really need any.

"How far down are we?" Harris asked, afraid to take his eyes off the creature in case it disappeared.

"Five hundred feet," came Stria's hushed reply. "It's beautiful, isn't it?" Beautiful wasn't the word he would've used, but he understood what she meant; they were the first humans to ever see life on another world: moving, glorious, alien life.

"Consistent undulations that do not correspond to any undersea currents," Stria continued. "We have a self-propelled organism. And I think if I'm seeing this correctly, there's some kind of mouth, perhaps? Near the edge, there, see it?" Harris looked where her gloved finger pointed at the screen.

"A small slit, yes, I see that. Unclear whether it's a mouth, a nostril, or even the creature's eye," he confirmed gruffly.

That came out harsher than I meant it to. Pull it together, man. You've worked with many other scientists before. This is no different. No different at all.

Stria smacked her helmet. "Of course! I'm thinking too much like an Earthling. I can't believe you caught that. You're right, that slit could be anything! We need more information before I can say with any certainty what it is."

Maybe Harris will be more valuable than merely extra muscle out here. After all, he saw what I didn't. And she was supposed to be the one trained in logical analysis. Could he actually help her be a better scientist? She risked a glance at him, but only met the smoggy clouds of Titan in his visor.

Harris, for his part, tried not to be insulted by the fact that she'd seemed surprised that he'd seen possibilities she hadn't.

*Another reason I can't let myself get carried away. She doesn't even think we're equals. Is it because I never went to college? Or because I'm a military man, and she thinks my only skills are moving heavy equipment and barking out orders? Even after I opened up to her last night, I'm **still** not good enough.*

"Well," he said, drawing a long breath to hide his displeasure, "it looks like we have something definite to share with the rest of the team now."

Stria squealed and shushed him as another of the creatures came into view on the screen. "It's not alone! Whatever it is, there's more than one of it!" she cried in delight, happy to get it all on tape.

The creatures kept their distance from one another, but seemed to undulate to the same mysterious rhythm. The second creature was the mirror-image of the first, except slightly longer. They stayed well below the surface of the Mare, and were out of camera range within twenty minutes of coming into view.

Stria and Harris watched and waited for two more hours, but no other creatures appeared. Leaving the probe to fend for itself in the murky depths, Stria walked to the far shore, mapping several ancient ripple patterns. She stopped every so often to draw one in her notebook as precisely as possible.

To her great annoyance, Harris followed her around the lake until it was time to pack up for the day. She felt like he was babysitting her, and she resented it.

By the time they crammed everything into the rover, Stria was confident that the original creature had been no fluke, and was excited about the possibility of a whole colony of creatures living below the inky sea's surface. But there were so many questions left to answer: *What did they eat? How did they breathe? Did they use some form of sonar to find their way in the black methane and ethane mixture that made up their home?*

She thought through all the possibilities on the way back to base, since Harris had stiffly offered to drive them, but was no closer to answering any of her questions by the time they went through the refining room.

She was beginning to wonder if three years would give her enough time to answer anything.

"Well, I'm glad today's expedition wasn't a waste of time," Harris began awkwardly. "I mean, it was good that we saw more of those...things...out there. Now that we're back inside, though, I should find Jala and start on a few tasks I've neglected around the station."

Why am I explaining myself to this woman? It doesn't matter to her what I do, he thought irritably. *And now that we're back inside the station, my job is done. Another civilian protected, nothing more.*

A strange look crossed Stria's face. "Oh, I thought I might ask you to help me review the footage in the lab. I was kind of hoping you'd be able to help me identify the various features of the organism's body. Your feedback about the creature today was surprisingly useful."

She looked at him appealingly, not wanting to be alone right now, and feeling ashamed of herself for being such an idiot. Why should it matter to her how Harris spent the rest of the afternoon? They'd been together for several hours already. And she didn't really need his help with the images, but for some reason she couldn't define, she wasn't quite ready to part with him yet.

Harris squared up his shoulders and lifted his chin a little higher.

"On one condition," he barked, coming across a little more sternly than he'd intended. "Only if I'm considered an equal partner in your research, and any discoveries I make about the creatures are credited to me."

There, that will tell me if she's ready to see me as a fellow human being with a brain, or as nothing more than a brain-dead bodyguard. Not that I care about her opinion of me either way.

Unknowingly, he'd arched his eyebrows hopefully at the end of his ultimatum, making it sound more like a request than an angry test of Stria's character. She readily agreed, embarrassed at how happy she was to be spending more time with the Assistant Commander.

Her scientific integrity demanded that she give credit where credit was due, anyway. She tried to hide her giddiness as she led him to the lab, clumsily jamming the memory stick into the video screen's data reader. *Harris is in the lab with me. Harris is in the lab with me.* It was all she could think about, in spite of herself.

Without their bulky spacesuits to keep them apart, Stria could once again smell the Assistant Commander's welcoming pine cologne. The narrow bench wasn't really designed for two people, and in order to not fall off the edge, Harris had to slide so close to Stria that they were constantly touching.

Her warm breath kept hitting the base of his neck. *I don't know how long I can pretend to focus on these pale, slinky worm-things,* he thought painfully. *There's no way I'll be able to maintain any sense of professionalism if I stay here any longer.*

But he couldn't make himself leave. So he sat there, in silent misery, fighting an internal battle with himself over the first woman he'd been attracted to in years.

Stria was determined to do what she'd said they were going to do, no matter how distracting Harris' nearness was. She barely had room to turn toward him without touching her face to his. He was so close her skin prickled. So very, tantalizingly close. She breathed in his scent, had no choice really, and only hoped she was having the same effect on him that he was having on her.

Breaking this heady spell, Harris called her attention to something suspended in the far left-hand corner of the screen. Intrigued, Stria zoomed in as much as she could without losing the image's integrity.

"What do you think that looks like?" Harris asked, indicating an object roughly fifty feet below the eel-like animals they'd been tracking at the lakeside.

Stria felt slightly ill. It looked for all the world like a spacesuit suspended in the Mare's depths.

"I thought you said Dr. Thompson's body had been incinerated?" she rasped, voice hushed with the horror of it all. At least Harris had been telling her the truth. Not that she doubted him, but last night it had all seemed a little too fantastic to be real.

"It was—I was there! And I was there for Dr. Kamura's incineration, too," he whispered tersely back.

"Then who is that?" Stria asked, turning wide, frightened eyes to her companion.

"I have no idea," he whispered, shaken to the core. There were only two runners. Only two. So what was going on here?

Not sure what else to do, Stria said a quick prayer over the new body and silently prayed that there wouldn't be any more unsettling discoveries.

The dinner chime sounded, making her jump slightly and upending Harris from the bench. Quickly pulling himself up, he looked around to make sure no one else had seen anything. The last thing he wanted was a few pairs of prying eyes coming over to see what had happened. "Shut that thing down, quickly," he urged in a tight voice.

He was worried that Reid was already suspicious of the scene they were causing, and it was decided they'd sit at separate tables at dinner, pretending nothing unusual had happened.

☆☆☆☆☆☆☆☆☆

Reid Everly was hard at work in his lab, poring over slides of microscopic life unfolding before his loving gaze. He was busy notating the unique, and previously unknown, color variations of the titanogranaticus reidii major. He'd named the tiny life he'd discovered after himself, of course! Suddenly, a gruff voice interrupted his careful studies.

He looked up fiercely. *Do these people have no respect? One would expect fellow scientists to understand the value of quiet study!* He looked for the source of the disturbance, and much to his unhappy surprise saw Harris Adley in one of the labs.

What is that fool doing? Playing at being a scientist? He was sitting so close to newcomer Dr. Reese he was practically in her lap. *Disgraceful! I'll have to speak to Jala about keeping her subordinates in line. What kind of operation is she running up here?*

He fussily shoved a pair of noise-canceling earphones on his head and tried to get back to work. He struggled to focus on his precious bacteria, however, and kept returning to the image of Harris in one of the labs. He was desecrating the sanctity of scientific research!

Not that Reid was jealous; he was far too concerned with his academic work for that, but he did have strong feelings about Harris' place in society, and people like him. He didn't even have a degree!

And for Harris to think he had a chance with someone who had a Doctorate...the very idea was preposterous! The Assistant Commander belonged to the "masses"—people who were destined to be led by the higher-minded and more intelligent scientists. And who did the masses owe their lives to?

Scientists, that's who. The very scientists who'd found the cures for a myriad of diseases and plagues. The scientists who'd discovered how to purify water, make food safe to store, and who discovered and refined interplanetary travel and colonization. It was the scientists who mattered, no one else.

Smiling darkly to himself, Reid got back to work, annoyed to hear the dinner bell moments later. There was so much to do and he was running out of time to do it in. He finished up his notes as quickly as he could, but realized he'd be pretty late for the evening meal. It was a small price to pay for the greatest discovery in history.

14: Agitation

Kirby was the first to arrive at dinner, rushing in like a whirlwind. Ivy noted to Zevon how out of character it was for her to be early, let alone rush anywhere, making them both wonder what had happened to their unflappable engineer.

"What do you think's the matter?" Ivy whispered, though no one would've been able to hear her with all the noise in the kitchen anyway.

Zevon furrowed his brows. "Maybe she's had a bad comm from home? Knowing there's nothing she can do from up here would be pretty rough."

"That's true…I guess I figured it was probably Drake getting to her again." Ivy's light tone masked the anger she felt remembering her own most recent encounter with the man.

Just thinking about it made her skin crawl. He'd trapped her in the hallway after dinner one night when she was heading back to her room. Drake told Ivy how pretty she was, how long he'd admired her, and what did she say to a little dessert in his room?

Ivy knew Drake (and other men like him) well enough to understand what he was really asking, and she very quickly turned him down. All the same, he didn't move. She was pinned, his hands flat against the wall on either side of her face, his breath uncomfortably close.

"Back off, Drake, I'm not interested," she'd hissed. But he seemed to think she was playing hard to get.

"Now honey, don't tease me like that. I know you're attracted to me, too," he'd smiled (seductively?) at her. All she felt was disgust.

Grabbing his wrists, she'd twisted them as hard as she could in opposite directions, and had been able to free herself before he could do any real damage. She sighed heavily at the memory and tried to focus on plating tonight's meal.

Ever since the "incident" as Ivy called it in her mind, Zevon had volunteered to serve Drake's meals so she didn't have to interact with him. He'd also volunteered to walk her to her room on nights she didn't have anyone else to walk with. She'd been deeply impressed by his willingness to step up on her behalf, though she'd never told him so.

Her thoughts brought her back to the question she'd kept asking herself ever since that night. *What if it happens again?* Ivy wasn't so sure she'd be able to overpower Drake if it ever came down to it.

She shot a quick glance at Zevon plating dinner. He was so

strong—but Drake was, too. Would he be able to protect her if Drake got physical again? Was it fair to expect Zevon to look out for her?

I'm probably just overreacting. I'm sure Drake would never do anything that...that...vile. He just likes to show off. He wouldn't have passed the psych eval if he were actually capable of hurting someone, right?

She'd gone crying to Zevon shortly after the incident had happened, and had brokenly told him everything. He'd been so warm and comforting and safe. But not even he knew how badly she'd been shaken by the whole ordeal.

Kirby's problems were forgotten for the moment, and dinner service began, without a single thought for Michael Kinney or his untimely death.

✫✫✫✫✫✫✫✫✫

Stria was so nervous she could barely eat the delicious meal in front of her, and was paranoid all through dinner that Jala was watching her. She practically ran to her room as soon as they were released for the evening, and didn't even acknowledge Harris on the way out.

She'd finally started to feel better about being on Titan, only for this to happen. She didn't want to start having panic attacks up here, or worse, end up like the suddenly growing number of runners.

Don't let me fall apart up here, she prayed silently in her room. *Keep me together, keep me together, please, God, keep me together.*

If only God didn't feel so incredibly far away up here...

☆☆☆☆☆☆☆☆☆

Reid indecorously pulled Commander Shan away from her table as the dessert plates were being set out, interrupting her in mid-sentence. And she was in the middle of a fascinating story about the time she'd single-handedly saved a team of astronauts from an unexpected meteor shower during her first assignment on Mars, too.

"I need to speak to you about a very critical matter," he breathed, puffing out his chest importantly. He'd pouted all through dinner and wasn't about to squander the opportunity to air his grievances to the Commander.

He propelled her toward a potted apple tree, which seemed a little more appropriate for a tête-a-tête than the doorway of the dining room.

"This had better be good," the Commander growled. "I am not accustomed to being torn away from dinner before I've even had a chance to eat my dessert." She glowered menacingly at him, but it was lost on Dr. Everly.

"Do you have any idea what I saw today?" he spluttered, struggling to keep his voice at a reasonable level.

"None whatsoever," Shan replied, frowning up at him. She always forgot how tall Reid was—she normally only saw him hunched over his microscope or a dinner plate.

She'd always assumed he used the gym—everyone here did from time to time—but it only registered tonight how muscled his lean arms were beneath his uniform. She recognized that he could pose a legitimate threat to the station's crew if he wanted to. She adopted a more serious look and prompted him to continue.

"Nothing less than YOUR subordinate cozying up to one of the new arrivals in the labs today! Is that something that is to be tolerated on this station? I expect to work in an environment that is free from distraction, where I can perform up to my highest levels—without being subjected to tawdry romantic displays in one of the science labs! If that is what interests your Assistant Commander, let him do it behind closed doors!" Red-faced and shaking with rage, Reid had to take a breath before he could go on.

Jala Shan took advantage of the momentary pause to assure him that she would have a conversation with Harris Adley about his inappropriate behavior. Satisfied for the moment, Reid huffed off to the sanctuary of his room.

Although Jala was truly disappointed in Adley's performance with Stria at the lab (if Reid could be believed), she was even more surprised by how quickly Reid's temper had escalated in such a short time.

In his two years here, he'd never shown any emotion other than disdain for those he thought below him, which was basically everyone else on the station.

She'd begun to think of him as an android devoid of all feeling, instead of a living, breathing human being. Commander Shan realized with a shock that she really didn't know much about Dr. Everly, and for the first time found herself wondering what he might be capable of.

It made her question how much she knew about anyone on the station. What were any of them capable of? Even Harris—who'd been so solid for the past seven years, was showing some very un-Harris-like behaviors lately.

Shaking her head, she trudged back to the dining room to have a talk with her second-in-command, but an urgent communication from NASA pulled her away. She wondered if they'd been able to contact the shuttle that was supposed to arrive next year. It had been too long without any communication from that ship, and Jala was getting worried.

15: The Next Shuttle

Misty could tell that Kirby wasn't herself during dinner, and politely declining Kaden's offer to play pyramids, she pulled her friend aside for a private chat before Kirby could escape to her room.

"Is everything alright, Kirby?" she asked with concern, motioning her to a set of chairs far enough away from the group playing games to have a quiet discussion.

Although older than Misty by several years, Kirby relied heavily on the younger woman's friendship. In fact, she was probably closer to Misty than anyone else on the station. Drake would never be someone Kirby told things to, of course, and while Ivy and Zevon were great, they didn't have much in common. It had been surprisingly difficult to find things to talk to them about that didn't involve food.

And, out of necessity, Commander Shan and Adley were a little removed from everyone else, and didn't exactly invite heart-to-heart chats with their crew members.

So it was with relief that Kirby unburdened herself to her friend.

"Just before dinner, I got a comm from my parents. Something happened to my sister, Taren..." Kirby blinked rapidly a few times to clear away the tears that were trying to fall.

"Taren's the one who joined NASA, right?"

"Yeah," the older woman's mouth formed a sad little half-smile. "She always wanted to be like her big sister..." The tears were really threatening to fall now.

"What happened, Kirby? Is she ok?"

"Her shuttle is missing!" Kirby sobbed, unable to stem the tide of grief this time.

"Missing? But how? I didn't realize she'd even been cleared for a mission."

"Neither did I! She wanted it to be a big surprise, and made my parents promise not to say anything. Somehow, she managed to get herself assigned to the final shuttle coming to Titan. Taren thought it would be great fun to show up when the shuttle gets here next year and yell 'Surprise!' and have a good laugh.

"She's legit, though—I mean, she's a really good chemist, and they wanted someone to do more detailed chemical analyses than anything that's been done up here so far."

"And you didn't know she was planning on coming here until now?"

"No—my parents only told me because of what happened to the shuttle. If it hadn't been lost, they never would've told me she was coming. They wanted to honor Taren's wish to keep it a secret. I guess NASA's lost the ability to communicate with the ship and can't track their flight path anymore. For all I know, Taren could be dead!"

"Unless we hear that she is, let's not assume the worst," Misty urged, placing a comforting hand on her friend's arm. "After all, no shuttle yet has ever gotten lost on the way to Titan, right? We all made it here safely! And you know how banged up that shuttle is in the bay—and it still got here in one piece. Commander Shan will do everything she can to make sure that shuttle makes it to Titan."

"I wish there were some way I could talk to her to know she was alright," Kirby sniffed. "She kept sending me cryptic messages—now I know it's because she was sending them from the shuttle on the way here. That's so like her to stay awake for the seven-year flight and keep comming me just to keep up her secret. I had no idea!"

"Not knowing what's happening is always the worst part," agreed Misty. "But don't give up on her yet. Or the Commander. Taren will be here right on time next year, you'll see!"

Kirby wished she had Misty's optimism and promised she'd try not to believe the worst. But she had a strong feeling she'd never see her sister again.

16: Buried Secrets

A few days after Dr. Kinney's death, the space station was humming along happily without him, almost as if he'd never even been there. Kirby had her own troubles to worry about, and the rest of the crew were just as preoccupied.

Ora was all for professionalism in the face of unexpected hardship, but she felt this was a little extreme. Every time she attempted to broach the subject of Michael's death, she was met with a cold shoulder, no matter who she spoke to.

The only information she'd been able to piece together was the fact that Kirby'd initially questioned whether the death was accidental, and that Misty never wanted to see another dead body for as long as she lived.

The attitude on this station was decidedly odd, and even though everyone seemed to be telling the truth about what had happened, Ora felt sure there was more to the story.

✫✫✫✫✫✫✫✫✫

Harris and Stria were supposed to spend an entire day mapping out more of Kraken Mare, but they decided to spend today in the lab instead. They'd only made it halfway through the lake's video feed after the shock of discovering the spacesuit.

Stria welcomed the chance to spend a few more hours in Harris' steady, soothing presence, although it was partly because she was afraid to review the rest of the footage by herself. Seeing the body, even though it was only on video, had upset her pretty badly, far more than merely hearing about Michael's death had done.

She'd been haunted by nightmares of the dead all night and was awake well before dawn Earth time, but she was determined to keep a brave face in front of Harris. She snagged an extra cup of coffee at breakfast this morning, and was sipping away pensively when Harris strode into the lab.

Taking one look at Stria, it was obvious she hadn't slept well; he could see faint circles lingering under her eyes. He'd spent most of last night regretting watching the footage with her—and reproaching himself (again) for ever telling her what had happened in the first place. But then, it would have been worse if she'd seen…it…without knowing anything ahead of time. Still, if he could undo it all, he would.

At least she didn't seem to be as condescending toward him as she was before. *Not that that's anything to feel good about,* he scolded himself. It was useless to be attracted to her—it couldn't end well. But it was already too late…he was falling for her and there was nothing he could do to stop it now.

"Ready to see what's on the rest of that tape?" Stria asked, faking an enthusiasm she didn't feel.

"Let's get down to it," he agreed, resisting the impulse to put his arm around her waist as they squeezed themselves onto the bench again today. They were so close, Harris didn't even have to lean in to whisper, "I think Reid is watching us."

Stria tried to look without seeming to. "You don't think he knows about what we've seen, do you?"

"I don't know—but I'm not in the mood to take chances."

Seeing that Reid was absorbed in his work again (or at least pretending to be), Harris quickly locked the lab door. He could never tell what was going on in Reid's head, and wouldn't put anything past him.

Stria was scrolling the video forward in time when Harris sat down. Another idea struck him, and he asked Stria to pause the tape.

He pulled the giant potted fern from its place in the corner over to the worktable—hiding the screen from anyone walking past.

"Finally give that fern something useful to do. Ok, let's begin again," he grunted in his usual economy of words. It conveyed to Stria, now that she was getting to know him better, a pragmatic attitude toward life, and she was glad to see he wasn't frightened like she was.

As they watched the camera pan from left to right scanning the darkness, Stria's jaw dropped and she turned disbelieving eyes toward Harris. "I see it, too," he said grimly.

There was a second body in the Mare.

Impulsively, he gave her hand a reassuring squeeze—he didn't like how she'd looked this morning, and he was prepared to physically keep her from running out of the station if he had to. At least with his hand on hers, she couldn't bolt.

Then a better thought came to him—what safer place to watch the footage than in Stria's own room? The walls (like all the rooms) were soundproofed, the only window looked out onto Titan and not inward to the station, and they could at least be comfortable instead of crammed onto a bench meant for one.

"We can't review the rest of this footage here," Harris said gravely in Stria's ear. "I'll get us some coffee and we can watch the rest of it in your room."

He felt her body relax, and the death-grip she'd had on his hand loosened a bit.

"That's a good idea," breathed Stria, quickly connecting the dots. She started to jump up, but Harris held her on the bench. "Slow and steady," he murmured. "We don't want to arouse Reid's suspicions."

Or anyone else's, he thought, immediately thinking of Jala. She was already concerned that Stria and Harris were getting too close to each other, and had given him a gentle reprimand for it at dinner. He didn't blame her—he'd been reprimanding himself constantly over his irrational attraction to the scientist. But he couldn't leave Stria alone now—not when they'd just discovered another body in the Mare.

In spite of her protests, Harris was worried she was still too fragile to be left alone for too long with a thing like this on her mind. When it came right down to it, *he* was too fragile to handle the shock by himself. He wouldn't admit it, but he was glad he hadn't made these discoveries on his own.

It was strangely comforting to have someone to talk everything over with, even if it was only a condescending scientist who felt he was beneath her. Not that he forgave her attitude, not for a minute! But he didn't think it was necessarily because of him—it seemed more like a barrier protecting her from being hurt.

Well, he had plenty of patience, and time, and he had no intention of hurting her. Maybe she'd eventually come around. He could already see she was attracted to him (though doing her best not to show it) and hoped she wouldn't let her fear win out.

As nonchalantly as possible, they both rose from the bench, trying to not move in any way that would attract attention from Reid's prying eyes. Stria slid the device holding their precious video into her sample bag, took a steadying breath, and carefully unlocked the door.

She walked back to her room, mindful of how painfully slow each step was. *I am calm, I am calm, I am calm. I will walk all the way back to my room. Head up, Stria. There is nothing out of the ordinary here, only a scientist taking a nice, normal walk in the corridor.*

She sighed with visible relief when she got to her door, and collapsed onto the bed when she made it inside. *How Harris has been able to keep secrets about dead bodies for years is beyond me. I've only known about things for a few days—and I'm about to lose it!*

Harris watched Stria depart, making sure she made it to her room, then walked casually to the dining room, took a full urn of coffee and a small pitcher of cream, and counted silently to twenty before approaching Stria's room from the opposite direction.

Though his face seemed to be devoid of all expression (his years of military training came in handy here), his thoughts were swirling around new possibilities.

Does Jala know about the other bodies? How could she not know? Why wouldn't she mention this? We've never kept secrets from each other before; at least, I never thought we had.

He'd barely gotten to Stria's door, still wrapped in his own thoughts, when she yanked him inside with surprising strength.

"I thought you'd never get in here!" she hissed, almost spilling coffee all over them both as she propelled him to the chair.

"You were supposed to be following right behind me!"

"I didn't want anyone getting suspicious," he replied slowly. "I mean, what would they have thought if we both left the lab at the same time and snuck off to your room together in the middle of the morning?"

Stria blushed, hoping he couldn't see it. She knew what she would've thought. "You're right," she said quickly, to cover her embarrassment. He wasn't even looking at her anyway, she realized, somewhat disappointed.

Distractedly, he poured their coffee into the two cups Stria offered, and absentmindedly stirred in some cream. She got the video feed queued up and was about to run the tape again when Harris' voice stopped her.

"I've been thinking," he said in his slow, ponderous way, looking at her for the first time since getting dragged into her room.

"How do we know those bodies are scientists? What if they're members of the construction crew? They were gone by the time Jala and I arrived, and anything could've happened before we came. I think we'd better examine both for as much detail as possible to see if we can figure out exactly who's been swimming in the Mare."

Stria began giggling hysterically. "Swim-swim-swimming!" she said, between giggles. "Swimming! Having a fun day at the beach!"

Harris watched her through narrowed lids—she'd dissolved into a fit of laughter on the bed, and he wondered if the strain had finally pushed her completely over the edge.

His second thought was that he was grateful they were in here, where no one could hear her hysterical laughter, instead of in the glass-enclosed lab.

"Stria!" he bellowed. He wondered if this was a good time to slap her—he'd never slapped a civilian before, but according to space station standards it was an approved method of shocking a hysterical person back to reality.

Though he'd attempted to sound commanding and in-charge, Stria heard the concern in his voice—the undercurrent of fear that she was losing her sanity.

She took a couple of deep breaths and forced herself to return his gaze, holding on to the little bit of stability that his presence brought. He was in this with her, every step of the way. She wasn't alone.

Not that she was about to go throwing herself in his arms or anything, like some old-fashioned damsel-in-distress, but she was glad that she didn't have to face this awful reality by herself. It was nice to have a shoulder to lean on.

"I'm alright, really," she managed to say. "I just thought it was funny, that's all. They couldn't really go swimming in that frozen concoction, you know, and I started thinking how silly they would have looked diving into the Mare."

She felt herself slipping toward hysteria again.

No, no, no...don't think about that. Think about Harris and his warm, brown eyes. So concerned, wanting so much for me to be ok. He's rooting for me; he's on my side for some reason. Even though I haven't treated him very well, he still wants things to work out for me. Why does he care so much?

Harris pulled his chair closer to the bed, drawn by something in Stria's eyes. She'd let down her walls for a second, but they quickly went back up as she abruptly blurted, "I suppose it goes without saying—but I'll say it anyway—you can't tell Commander Shan about what we've found. She never told you about anyone actually being in the Mare, and I don't trust her. Even if she didn't know about the bodies, we have to keep this between us."

Stria searched his steady brown eyes nervously; she didn't know how close he was to Jala, and wondered if she could trust him to keep secrets from his Commanding Officer. Afterall, he'd spent more time with Jala Shan than anyone else on the Station. And how long had he known Stria? *Not long enough to matter,* she thought bitterly.

"If you think it best, then I won't say anything to her; though if she is aware of these other bodies, I'd like to know why she didn't tell me. It just doesn't make sense."

"If she knew and didn't tell you, then I think it's all the more reason to keep it our secret for now. Anyway, we don't know enough yet to involve other people," Stria insisted.

"Alright—I'll keep it quiet for now, but if we get to a point where it becomes necessary for her to have this information, I'm going to tell her," he stubbornly replied. Duty mattered to Assistant Commander Adley far more than it did to most people these days.

Accepting this as the closest thing to a promise of secrecy she was going to get, Stria rewound the tape to the sighting of the first body and they examined it closely, Harris finding he needed to sit on the bed next to Stria to see everything.

17: Complications

For the past week, Jala had been unable to contact the shuttle to ensure it was on the correct path, and she was beginning to get nervous. It was early November by Earth's calendar, and the clock was ticking.

Although it was only ten a.m. Earth time, Commander Shan had already been trying to hail the wayward shuttle for several hours and hadn't gotten lucky so far. To make matters worse, there was a cosmic storm today, garbling transmissions even further. She was beginning to wonder if she'd be able to direct the wayward ship after all.

Shan wasn't the type to give up easily, but she doubted if she was going to get through until after the storm had passed—if then, depending on how close they were. Her window to act was getting smaller and smaller with each passing minute.

Rubbing her eyes, and readjusting her disheveled black bun, she decided to take a coffee break and work out the kinks in her legs with a few laps around the station. *Nothing like a brisk run to get the blood flowing again and re-energize the brain!*

And the coffee wouldn't hurt, either. Zevon knew the Commander liked her coffee as strong as possible, and always had a special pot brewing just for her in the dining room. She congratulated herself again on getting him up here. Not only was he a great chef, but he was also fun to have around, and there weren't many people that Jala Shan truly enjoyed. Especially not up here.

She stretched out her arms and legs, completed two quick laps around the inner ring of the station, then made her way briskly to the dining room for a jolt of caffeine. She was rounding a curve in the hallway when she thought she saw Harris going the other direction with a pot of coffee. Her curiosity piqued, Jala followed at a distance, always keeping out of sight. She wanted to see where Harris was going, and was afraid that if he saw her, he'd change his course.

Much to her displeasure, she saw him head directly for Stria's room with a determined step.

Jala hadn't been able to spend as much time with Harris lately because of this shuttle issue—and the need to keep Stria from losing her head up here in space, of course—so she'd been relegated to seeing him only at mealtimes.

She was hesitant to bring up Stria again, and felt weak for avoiding the subject, but she needed to stay on Adley's good side. Truth be told, she was afraid of pushing him too far and losing his friendship.

And, she rationalized, it wasn't like he was overtly flirting with the woman. Harris had never overstepped his bounds when Jala had seen them together, but still...something about their relationship nagged at her. Maybe it was how close they seemed to be after such a short time together—sharing secrets already it seemed to her. But what kind of secrets could the two of them possibly have?

In spite of herself, Commander Shan felt a sharp pang at the thought that he could truly be falling for Stria. She was all wrong for him! Not his type at all. He needed someone as strong and as powerful as he was; someone who was his equal in every way. A woman like Jala, when you came right down to it.

And secretly, if she were honest with herself, hadn't she begun to picture Adley as more than just her second-in-command lately? Before Stria had come, it seemed that she and the Assistant Commander had grown closer through the ordeal of the runners, and Jala had found herself leaning on him more than she'd relied on anyone in a very long time.

Maybe it was a silly flash of jealousy, after all—petty, childish jealousy. Of course she was being unreasonable. Harris wasn't the type to lead anyone on, least of all a temporary scientist, who was here and gone before you knew it.

Reluctantly, she turned her thoughts back to the errant shuttle, and returned unhappily to her room to attempt contact one more time.

☆☆☆☆☆☆☆☆☆

"There it is!" Stopping the tape at the point they saw the first body yesterday, Stria zoomed in as much as she could while still holding on to enough detail to keep things recognizable.

"Unfortunately, the visor is frozen over—I can't see whose face is behind it," Harris growled in irritation. "There's no way we're going to be able to tell who these people were without some kind of additional information—like an employee log for the construction crew or NASA's records of missing persons."

"Let me see if I can zoom closer—maybe we'll still be able to tell something from the spacesuit?" Stria suggested hopefully, remembering at the last second that none of the spacesuits had names on them, only the uniforms everyone wore inside the station.

Unsurprisingly, a closer inspection didn't reveal any new details, but they were able to guesstimate how tall the dead body had been in life. "Well, on to body number two, I guess," Harris said, not trying to be flippant, but sounding like it all the same.

Again, nothing useful emerged from their inspection of the second corpse, still enshrined in the frozen spacesuit it went into the Mare with. They made another guesstimate of the height and weight of body number two, and moved on with trepidation to the rest of the film.

Thankfully, no new bodies emerged from the depths, but Harris felt that two was more than enough.

18: New Suspicions

Kirby and Drake rushed out of the dining room as soon as it was acceptable to leave after dinner, and Kaden was eager to start up a game of Pyramids (again!) with Misty, Zevon, and Ivy.

They'd played Pyramids nearly every night since they'd arrived here. Not that Ora didn't like the game, but it was quite clear that the foursome wasn't really looking for anyone else to join their tight-knit little group.

Once again, she felt her age, and wondered what she was going to do with her time tonight. She was loving her work here—she'd had a renewed sense of purpose since Michael's death and wanted nothing more than to carry on the work he'd begun as a way to honor his memory.

Not that anyone else seemed to care much about that. They'd barely even mentioned him in the intervening weeks since his death, and you'd never know by looking at the rest of the station's inhabitants that anything unpleasant had ever happened.

Ora couldn't understand their attitude, and it made her feel even more alone than she already did. Sadly, her fears from the first night had come true—she'd found no friends here, and now her only actual colleague was dead.

Not that the others weren't nice enough—they were, and Ora had been invited to join them several times for games, but she always felt like a third wheel. Even Stria, *timid, shy little Stria* was the center of Assistant Commander Adley's protective attention.

No, life on the station hadn't been all it was cracked up to be, and Ora was beginning to regret her decision to come. *At least it's only three years,* she thought tiredly.

She decided to go to the library for a change, which she'd been avoiding since Michael's death. It felt odd to be here, in the very room where...

In the end, she couldn't do it, and walked dejectedly to her own room, preparing to go to bed early once again. At least her days were filled with interesting work. *If only the nights didn't drag on so long,* she thought wistfully.

☆☆☆☆☆☆☆☆☆

"The rose garden—again? You really don't have much creativity when it comes to meeting spots, do you, Drake?"

"Look, Kirby, you're the one who commed me in a panic this morning, so I'm really not interested in your sarcasm right now. It's the rose garden or nothing. Now tell me what's gotten you all upset."

Kirby knew she was being unfair. It was just her anxiety about Michael's death that made her lash out. She paced back and forth, touching the silky rose petals as she went, trying to compose her thoughts.

"You know how I was thinking maybe Dr. Kinney's death wasn't some sort of tragic accident?"

Uh-oh. Not this again. Drake arched his eyebrows in irritation.

"And **you** know how I feel about that, right? Why would someone go to all the trouble to make it look like an accident if it wasn't?" Anger was making his voice rise.

"Shhhh," Kirby hissed. "Keep your voice down. I've been thinking a lot about this, and I'm pretty sure Michael was another runner. You know, like Dr. Kamura. Except he didn't go wandering outside, he just decided to climb a bookshelf and fell off instead."

"Now why on Titan would he go and do something stupid like that?"

"Space sickness, of course!" Kirby stared at him like it was obvious. *Why couldn't Drake understand this?*

"Maybe he was having one of those hallucinations Dr. Thompson always warned us about—you know, where you think you're back on Earth rock climbing or something, but really you're just trying to climb a bookshelf on a research station in the middle of the solar system?"

She looked triumphantly at Drake, as if that explained it all perfectly.

"How does that make any more sense than him just falling after trying to find a book? You're reading way too much into this, Kirby. It might be high time you got off this tangerine cluster of a moon and went home."

"You never looked at the books that were scattered around him, did you? Well, I did! And I can't get them out of my head—they're there whenever I remember Michael's crumpled body. I swear, he never would've been reading romance books!"

"How do you know what Mike secretly liked to read? Maybe he was a huge romance fan, for all we know."

"Drake, listen to yourself," Kirby sighed in exasperation. "Don't be a fool. We both know there's more to this story than just a fall. Now, my only question is, should I tell the others about my theory or not?"

Drake grabbed Kirby's arm roughly—he'd had enough of her foolish ideas for one night and her constant pacing was starting to get on his nerves.

"Do you want to panic everyone on this station? What good would it do to tell the others that some people can't hack it up here and go off and kill themselves, whether it's accidental or not?"

"I don't know, I don't know!" Kirby pushed her fingers through her blonde waves in exasperation, struggling to make sense of it all.

"We didn't say anything before, and it didn't seem to stop Michael from doing away with himself anyway. So, what good has keeping secrets done for us, Drake?"

Not much, he thought to himself, finally realizing where all this was going.

"No matter what you do, don't you dare go telling anyone else about this," he threatened, tightening his grip on her arm. "It won't do any good."

He glared into her fiery eyes until she finally agreed to keep her crazy theories to herself for a while. *It's too bad she doesn't save any of that fire for me,* he thought, eyeing her body hungrily.

Disgusted, she tossed her head. "Don't look at me that way. If we're finished here, you can let me go and I'll pretend we didn't have this discussion at all. Okay?"

Those eyes of hers. There has to be some way...

"Listen," he began desperately, hoping this would do the trick when nothing else had gotten Kirby on his side before.

"I've been working on something for a while, and it's...Jala doesn't know, so I'd appreciate it if you didn't say anything to her, or else she'll totally shut me down."

Kirby didn't want to hear any more of Drake's secrets, but with his hand wrapped tightly around her arm, she didn't have much choice. Her nostrils flared as he continued, uncertain.

"Uh...this project...it's...I've been repairing the old shuttle in the hangar," he rushed, trying to get the words out quickly before he lost his nerve. "And I wondered if you'd want to leave the station early with me and finally get away from this place. Together."

Even Drake's innocently hopeful glance looked smarmy and seductive to Kirby, and it made her skin crawl.

Horrified at the thought of being alone with her colleague on a shuttle for seven years, Kirby angrily yanked her arm from his grip.

Her mind reeled from the implications of what he'd just told her.

"You've been secretly repairing the shuttle for months, and never thought to say anything to anyone until now? Were you planning on running away by yourself? How selfish can you be?"

"But, I just asked you to go with me," he said, honestly confused by her hostility.

"Yeah, that's the problem!"

She was so upset, she didn't even have the energy to hurl one of her usual insults at Drake on her way out of the greenhouse.

Shaken and confused, he walked slowly to his room, telling himself what a fool he'd been to take Kirby into his confidence. She was never going to like him, let alone want him, and he'd probably just ruined his own chances of getting off the moon early by telling her about the shuttle. Of all the luck—he'd been assigned to the one station in the Universe where all the women were fickle and cold.

To make matters worse, he wondered if Kirby was right about Mike's death. If he'd succumbed to space sickness, maybe they *should* start telling the others the truth before it was too late.

Then a darker thought crossed his mind. Maybe someone *had* killed Mike. He knew that Reid, for instance, didn't miss him at all. He wasn't about to mention that idea to Kirby—she'd lose her mind up here for sure if she thought that were true.

But maybe once she cooled down, she'd end up changing her

mind about going with him—after all, every time somebody mentioned next year's shuttle, she looked like she was going to pass out, punch something, or both.

☆☆☆☆☆☆☆☆☆

Kaden had been feeling restless the last few days, and he wasn't sure why. It's not that he was getting tired of Misty, or of his work on the station. Far from it—he was like a kid in a candy store. Everything was so fascinating on this far-flung moon, and he loved seeing Saturn rise and set in the Titanean sky. It never got old.

And Misty—she was something else. He'd never met a woman he could talk to so easily, or about so many things. You'd never know she hadn't gone to college—at least he didn't notice any difference between them. She was quick-witted, with a sparkling smile and endless mysteries waiting to be discovered behind those gray eyes.

No, it wasn't the work or the company that was getting to him. It was the fact that there seemed to be a lot of secrets at this station, and he wasn't privy to any of them—yet. It made him feel like a little kid again, not big enough to be trusted with anything important.

He was irritated by the thought. It was obvious something was going on, but he couldn't figure out what.

*Why does everyone have to slink off for a special rendezvous all the time? I mean, Drake and Kirby are in the greenhouse so often you'd think **they** were the ones responsible for keeping the plants alive. And don't get me started on the way Harris and Stria creep around the station, thinking nobody's wise to what they're doing.*

Take tonight for instance—Kirby and Drake had run off to the greenhouse together right after dinner. He'd been under the impression that Kirby couldn't stand her coworker, but she sure wasn't acting that way now.

19: A Close Call

The last few weeks had passed fairly quietly, much to Stria's great surprise. In fact, things had become almost routine. She'd dutifully made notes about the eel creatures and spliced together a few minutes of video that Harris had deemed safe (no dead bodies in the frame) to send back to NASA.

It all had to go through Commander Shan, of course.

Lately, Harris had begun to wonder why it was so important for Jala to review everything before it was sent off to NASA. It had never crossed his mind before, but working so closely with Stria made him realize that it didn't make much sense.

Sure, it streamlined things a bit, but not really enough to justify routing everything through one person. And now that Harris knew there were two strange bodies in the Mare, he could no longer take everything at face value the way he'd done before. In fact, if Drake, Kirby, and Misty hadn't backed up Jala's version of Michael's death, he'd be willing to doubt that, too.

✩✩✩✩✩✩✩✩✩

It had been a rough morning, and for a while there, Jala didn't think she was going to be able to pull it off. After all, it'd been tough sailing for the past few weeks, not getting anything but static when she tried to communicate with the shuttle that was not quite a year away.

But she'd done it! Finally catching a break, she'd been able to get a lock on the shuttle's navigation systems at last. It was all taken care of now, and she didn't need to worry anymore.

The shuttle was finally going where it was supposed to go. She'd comm NASA right after lunch and tell them the good news. But first, she wanted to find Adley and let him know.

And maybe she'd slip in a quick word about his poor choices toward Stria. He'd been spending more and more time with the attractive, young scientist lately, and it was beginning to leave a bad taste in her mouth.

The Commanding Officers had to set a good example for the crew and visiting scientists—something that Harris had always taken seriously until now. She couldn't understand it. He knew the folly of becoming romantically involved with someone on the space station. Besides, there'd be plenty of time for romance once they reached end-of-mission.

She was beginning to feel that it was high time Stria started exploring Titan in the company of the other scientists. Shan trotted briskly to Harris' room with a renewed sense of purpose, but he wasn't there.

20: Awkward Questions

The station's chefs were putting the final touches on lunch service. Ivy snuck a quick peek at Zevon's face. There was something she needed to tell him, but she'd been putting it off for a while now, afraid of how he'd react. She knew delaying the inevitable conversation wouldn't make it any easier to have, so it was now or never.

Taking a deep breath, Ivy summoned all her courage and said,

"Zevon, do you ever think about heading home early? I mean, I realize we're supposed to stay until end-of-mission, but lately, I've been thinking that maybe I'd like to go back on that shuttle next year with Reid. If Drake weren't up here with us, I don't think it would matter so much, but..." She dropped her eyes, thinking again about that awful night.

Zevon almost dropped the bowl of salad he was carrying.

"But...Ivy...what...what would I do without you?" he mumbled, his voice so low it was almost a whisper.

He couldn't help it—the words fell out of his mouth before he could stop them. He tried not to look her in the eye; it would be too painful to see the rejection he was sure would be reflected in them.

The shock of her hand on his whipped his head up. She gazed steadily at him, and with a small smile curving at the corners of her mouth, said, "Why, Zevon—I was kind of hoping you might want to go with me."

"Do you really mean that, Ivy? I've always dreamed, that is...I've always hoped..." As he floundered helplessly for the right words, Ivy realized that he was in love with her. She wondered now how she could have missed something so obvious—but then, it seemed that Zevon still hadn't caught on to the fact that she was just as in love with him.

"Of course I do! I don't know what I'd do without you, either. And the way you've looked out for me, ever since Drake...well, you're truly the most incredible man I've ever met, Zevon. I've known that for a long time." She looked up at him with those hypnotic green eyes, and he knew it was all over.

"I...I love you, Ivy. If you're ready to go home next year, then I'll go with you."

"Oh, Zevon, I'm so glad. I was so afraid you'd want to stay here without me."

"Never!"

Putting down the salad and pulling Ivy close, he kissed her with a passion that came from seven years of pent-up emotion.

✫✫✫✫✫✫✫✫✫

Harris Adley made the unusual move of ordering lunch in his room, and commed Stria to join him there, with a warning to not let anyone see her on the way. He knew Jala would notice his absence at lunch but he desperately needed to talk some things over with Stria.

Maybe he could tell Jala he'd been sick and stayed in his room all afternoon. That was at least plausible—Jala could tell he'd been a little off lately and he was almost out of excuses. She'd already talked to him once about his closeness to Stria, and if she wanted to think he was falling for the scientist, that'd be as good an excuse as any to be off his game, he supposed.

Once inside the soundproofed safety of his room, and settled comfortably into the armchair, Stria took a bite of creamy chicken pot pie and gave Harris time to figure out how to say what he wanted to say. She'd learned how to read him pretty well by now, and understood that he couldn't be rushed when there were important things to talk about. She didn't mind the silence; somehow, it felt peaceful, even when the things they had to discuss were anything but.

"I've been doing some research on my own," Harris said in his slow, deliberate style. "For one, I found out that everyone from the construction crew was accounted for—they all arrived safely back on Earth and NASA has solid confirmation that none of them went missing. So the two bodies we found in the lake can't be anyone involved in construction. That only leaves..."

"The scientists who've come and gone," Stria finished, deflated. Somehow, she was hoping that the bodies had ended up in the

Mare because of some construction accident, or a long-ago hatred that had already played itself out and couldn't hurt them anymore.

"That's the only conclusion that seems to fit, but I can't understand it. I know that the bodies can't be Dr. Kamura or Dr. Thompson, because I was with Jala when they were incinerated. So it must be the other two scientists who were supposed to leave right before Reid and Dr. Kinney arrived."

Stria puckered her forehead in thought. "But that doesn't make any sense. You all watched the ship leave, right? You know those two scientists were on the ship when it left, so is there anyone else it could have been?"

"There's absolutely no one else it could be—at the time, it was only me, Jala, Kirby, Drake, Misty Lee, Ivy, and Zevon. Reid and Dr. Kinney arrived about a month or so after the other ship left, so it was just us on the crew. Then no one else arrived until your group showed up."

"Well, that should be easy to confirm—can't we comm NASA and ask them who got off the ship?"

Harris smacked himself in the forehead. "I'm such an idiot! They haven't arrived back on Earth yet. I mean, they only left 2 years ago, which means they won't get back to Earth until 2105, so they've still got nearly five years left on their journey home."

"That does make things more complicated," Stria sighed. "It seems like the bodies have to be theirs, but it can't be them, because you stood there and watched them get in the ship and leave. This is impossible!"

Harris cut her off before she could say anything else, the words tumbling out so fast he started to stutter a little. It took a few moments before he was calm enough for Stria to understand him.

"I didn't stand there and watch the ship!" he finally managed to splutter. "None of us did! We watched it leave the atmosphere from the station. Jala was the only one who actually went to the ship. And Jala was the one who said...who said...she said..."

Stria tried to help him put his scattered thoughts into order.

"You mean Commander Shan is the only one who can confirm that anyone even got on that shuttle? And you only have her word for it that they were actually on the ship?"

"Yes," he groaned, "but I don't see why she'd lie about whether or not they got on the ship. It wouldn't make sense to invent a story like that. I know she would've told me if they'd never boarded the shuttle," Harris said adamantly.

"Well, maybe she was trying to protect you all. What if they attacked each other for some reason? Maybe it was simply two more examples of space sickness going really, really wrong, and she wanted to keep it from getting out."

Harris had to grudgingly admit that did sound like something the Commander would do, since he was already aware of two other times she'd lied to the crew for their protection.

"Okay, so if she did lie about them getting on the shuttle, then what would she do? I mean, if they'd injured each other so badly they couldn't make the journey back, or if somehow they were actually dead when she found them?"

"I suppose...I suppose she'd just say they left," he speculated.

"Each shuttle is programmed to take off automatically at a certain time, whether there are any passengers inside or not. So I guess it would make sense for Jala to say they'd gotten on the shuttle as planned, since all of us would see it leaving Titan's atmosphere anyway. But I still don't understand why she didn't tell me if that was the case. We always tell each other everything!"

Stria shot him a quick, panicked look.

"Except for my conversations with you, of course," Harris rushed to assure her.

"Maybe once you get used to lying about a thing, it's easier to do it again. I realize that I haven't been up here as long as everyone else, but I do think lying about the whole space sickness thing is doing a disservice to everyone at the station. Don't you think people have a right to know if they're in some kind of danger? Especially if that danger could come from someone they're working with! It's not too late to tell them what you know."

"I'm not sure I could do that," Harris squirmed under her intense gaze. "I still think the cost would be too high, and I'm not willing to risk any more lives on a hunch that knowing might be better than not knowing. After all, we haven't had any new incidents in two years. Unless Michael..." He stopped before he could go any further. He couldn't bring himself to believe that.

"OH!" Stria's eyes widened as a new possibility dawned on her, and she pointed wildly to their scattered notes about the creatures they'd seen in the Mare.

"What if the eel-creatures are able to come up to the surface? After all, both bodies were found in the Mare. What if they attacked the two men and pulled them in? Although we haven't been able to observe that behavior ourselves, it doesn't mean they couldn't, right?"

Stria shuddered slightly as she imagined gigantic eyeless, colorless eels wrapping their bodies around unsuspecting victims and pulling them beneath the dark waveless surface of the Mare.

"I don't know...I just...don't know." The way Stria outlined the story—both stories—made sense, and lying to protect her crew certainly sounded like something that Jala would do. And yet, there was something that didn't feel right about it.

Harris couldn't understand why Jala would lie to **him**. Sure, he could see her trying to protect the others by hiding the truth from them, but him? It wasn't merely his bruised ego talking—he knew Jala too well. They'd worked side-by-side for seven years.

He was beginning to realize how much he'd relied on Jala's word for everything. And now, for the first time, he wondered if that had been such a wise thing to do.

He knew he was missing something, and worried that if he didn't figure it out, more civilians would be harmed.

His thoughts darted anxiously between Michael's untimely death, the bodies in the Mare, and Jala lying to him about the scientists leaving Titan. Jala lying about space sickness, about space shuttles, about dead bodies.

To tell him, of all people, that they'd gone up in the shuttle when she knew they hadn't just didn't make sense.

Uncomfortably, Harris finally realized he wasn't going to figure anything out unless he confronted Jala. He felt he deserved to know why she didn't trust him enough to tell him what had really happened to the scientists.

And, unless Stria's murdering-eel theory was right (which Harris highly doubted), there was still one nagging question: how did both bodies end up in the Mare? It didn't add up; though he had no idea what did.

He quickly checked the clock; far too late to discuss these new uncertainties with Jala tonight. *First thing tomorrow then; she at least owes me that.*

21: Accusations

Breakfast the next morning looked more like a mutiny than a communal meal. Stria gingerly avoided Drake's table, where it was obvious a storm was brewing. Unfortunately for her, even though she sat as far away as possible, she could still hear every angry word.

Ivy and Zevon had retreated to the kitchen when things started to hit the fan, and were happily oblivious in their safe little bubble together. *If only I could do that, too,* Stria thought unhappily. She hated confrontation (though Harris might disagree), and her cheeks burned with embarrassment for everyone else.

"What I do on my own time is none of your business," she heard Drake say to probably Kaden—it was hard to tell who the remarks were directed to, because he glanced wildly around the table as he spoke.

"Come on Drake, let's not keep secrets around here," Kaden pushed. "I know you and Kirby are up to something. You're always sneaking off together!"

Bristling at the insinuation, Kirby pushed herself angrily from the table and stood up, towering over the still-seated geologist. "How dare you!" she spat, unwilling to be connected to Drake in even the slightest way.

"You have no idea what you're talking about, and I refuse to be insulted by a...a *scarecrow*!"

"Alright..." Kaden muttered, shocked by Kirby's sudden anger.

He'd never seen her temper flare up like this during his short time on the station, and was completely caught off guard. He decided to focus on Drake's solo, late-night trip to the hangar instead, hoping to get Kirby off his back.

"At least I know that Drake's been keeping secrets, because I saw him sneak off to the hangar one night after we all should've been in our rooms. So, what gives?"

Misty leaned forward curiously. Drake knew better than to be prowling around the station at night. *What was he thinking?*

Drake nervously ran his hands through his hair. Clearly, he hadn't been as clever about hiding his night-time activities as he'd thought.

Kirby shot her coworker a furious glance. *Of all the stupid, idiotic...he can't even keep his own secrets,* she thought irately. *And he's been lecturing* **me** *about keeping it together! I knew we should've told the truth from the beginning.*

"You might as well tell him, Drake," she huffed, "*all* of it." Sliding down into her seat, she braced herself for the inevitable fallout, and regretted, for the thousandth time, finding Dr. Kamura's body with her fellow engineer.

"Yes, I agree that would be for the best, Drake," Ora said gravely.

He'd almost forgotten she was seated at the table with them, but then, she wasn't really his type, so he tended not to notice her most of the time, anyway.

Realizing they weren't going to let it go until he told them the truth, Drake finally gave in.

"Listen, I don't want what I'm about to tell you getting to Jala and Harris," he said in exasperation, "because I know Commander Shan would shut me down, and I've only got a few more hours of work left before it's ready."

"Before what's ready?" Misty asked, suddenly confused about where all this was heading. She was fully expecting to hear he'd been sneaking off for some salacious reason.

"The shuttle," Kirby said, with a crooked grin on her face. Misty wasn't sure at first whether she was joking or not.

"The one in the bay?" Kaden asked. "With the huge pockmark in the nose?"

"That's the one," Drake sighed unhappily. *All this work down the drain for nothing. There's no way this many people will keep quiet. Half of them don't even like me!*

Breathing in deeply, Drake finally spilled one of his many secrets. He felt naked talking about it, like they'd somehow taken away something private and special and uniquely his. Having to reveal it in front of a hostile audience ruined everything.

"I've been working on rebuilding the shuttle in the hangar for the past year." He paused, letting the magnitude of what he'd been doing sink in.

Several gasps filled the dining room. Even Stria, huddled at her far away table, must've heard.

"You might as well come on over, Stria," he grudgingly offered. "I know you can hear us over there."

Reluctantly, she joined the group, just in time to hear Kaden's astonishment.

"Hold on—you've been sneaking around at night for a year and never managed to get caught by Jala?" Kaden asked, in awe of Drake's stealthy cunning. *What else is this man capable of?* he wondered.

"Never—and if she knew I was working on making that thing flight-worthy again, she'd put a stop to it." Drake glared at everyone at the table, hoping they understood how serious he was.

Seeing Misty's incredulous face, he added, "You know she would! Some misplaced idea of protecting us from ourselves and not creating a panic. I was planning on taking myself home as soon as it was ready to go. But now...since all of you know about it, that's going to be impossible."

"Yeah, it was so nice of you to plan on running away and leaving me to handle all of the station's systems and machines by myself!" Kirby accused.

"I did ask you to come with me..." Drake began, embarrassed to relive the humiliation of her turning him down in front of the group.

She brushed him off before he could finish. "We signed up for a ten-year mission—or did you forget that? Besides, I couldn't leave now even if I wanted to—my sister decided to surprise me and got herself assigned to the shuttle that's arriving in a few months."

"I had no idea," Drake shrugged, sure those weren't her only reasons for turning him down.

"Unfortunately, now you all know about the shuttle, which means, I guess, that I'll have to make room for those who'd like to leave early. But, I don't want everyone fighting over who gets to be on the return flight—this is a smaller shuttle, and there's not much room. Remember, another shuttle's coming next year, so some of you will have to be patient."

Ora seemed to be the only one who understood the narcissism behind Drake's actions, and she, alone of all the station's inhabitants, was genuinely outraged.

"Of all the selfish, short-sighted, idiotic plans!" she burst out. "Your idea was to leave the station without any engineers for the next four years and cavalierly hope everything worked out for the best? Because you couldn't handle life on the station any longer, you decided to sentence everyone else to a long, slow death?"

"Hey, back off! I've been up here for six years already. When you've been on this station for that long, on this orange creamsicle moon that hardly gets any sunlight, maybe you'll feel a little differently about doing what you have to do to stay sane. And besides, these systems have so many fail-safes that they'd keep working a good five to ten years after everyone was gone."

Kirby couldn't believe she was defending Drake, but she cut in with a terse, "Look, you don't know what happened to Dr. Kamura! And maybe if you'd been the one to find his body, you'd want to get off this moon, too!"

"What are you talking about, Kirby? Dr. Kamura returned to Earth," Misty questioned, bewildered by this new turn of events. She was just starting to wrap her head around the fact that Drake wanted off the station so badly that he'd secretly repaired the old shuttle to escape.

"No, Misty Lee, that's just something Jala said to calm everyone else down. I know for a fact he's dead because Drake and I found his body."

"But why would Jala lie like that?" Misty shook her head in disbelief. Commander Shan was always honest with them, even when it was tough. *Kirby must be mistaken. He has to be on that shuttle, safely heading back to Earth, which is what he wanted so much anyway.*

"She didn't want the rest of us to become like him," Drake suggested, grateful that the conversation was finally moving away from his clandestine repairs.

"What do you mean, 'become like him'?" Ora quizzed. Her intelligent mind was racing ahead, already putting several pieces of the puzzle together, while Kaden merely looked on in shocked silence.

"Are you insinuating it was an extreme form of space sickness?" she hazarded, and knew she was right when Kirby winced.

Drake nodded solemnly. "Now you know. That's why Jala was afraid to tell you all. She didn't want it to spread to the rest of the station like wildfire," he added, grateful in an odd way that he didn't have to keep this secret any longer.

"His face was all twisted up in agony and just frozen there. And the suit...there were gashes torn out of it everywhere," Kirby added, shivering, and Drake put a comforting, but unwanted, arm around her.

"I still see him some nights in my dreams," she gulped, pushing Drake's arm away.

"For two whole years I believed Dr. Kamura ran away and left us all here without a doctor. And now you're telling me that he didn't run away at all, but is actually dead? And that he died here, on Titan," Misty blurted.

A new idea struck her as she was speaking. "Wait a minute, you've known what happened for two years and you never told me before now? Didn't you trust me, Kirby?"

"Oh, Misty, it's not that I didn't trust you...but Jala swore us to secrecy, and I couldn't break that!"

Misty still felt like she'd been betrayed. Not that she didn't appreciate how Jala tried so hard to look out for everyone and keep them safe...but this made her feel like a child.

And it wasn't just Jala. Kirby was her best friend up here, and she'd kept this from her for two years! That hurt, deeply.

It upset everything she thought she knew about the crew, about Jala, and about space sickness itself. Could she trust herself to stay sane? Could she trust Kaden?

Misty suddenly felt sorry for the next bunch of scientists on their way here. It made everything worse knowing that one of them was Kirby's sister. She felt guilty for having enjoyed living on Titan so much, and sadly wondered if anything would ever feel the same again now that she knew the truth.

"I think we're forgetting the most important part," Stria timidly interrupted. She'd been so quiet the table forgot she was there, which sadly, wasn't unusual.

"Drake's managed to fix the shuttle." Turning to the man himself, she asked cautiously, "Have you really been able to get the nav systems working again? Oh, and does it have enough fuel to get back to Earth?"

"Yes," Drake confirmed. "It was designed to make a round-trip, but Commander Shan stepped in and said the exterior shields were too damaged to make re-entry. But I've checked and double-checked those shields with several different instruments, and they're solid. Sure, they're a little banged up, but they haven't been compromised in any way. The old girl can make it back home."

"And how many people can fit in the shuttle?" Stria tried to keep the excitement out of her voice. If only she could go home now, instead of having to wait even one more year. She'd do anything to get on that shuttle, even if it did mean seven years with Drake.

"It was designed for four people in cryosleep—but technically, two more people could fit on the shuttle if they were willing to stay awake for the seven-year ride home. It might be weird when it came time for the others to wake out of cryosleep and they saw that whoever stayed awake was seven years older while they remained the same age, but we'd all be back on Earth, so..."

"So, the question becomes," mused Kirby, glad to no longer be talking about Dr. Kamura, "if anyone else is willing to join you. I've already said I won't be heading back with you, so that frees up one spot on your little vacation trip."

"Remember, if anyone does want to leave, we can't say anything to Commander Shan, or Adley," he added, looking pointedly at Stria. "Don't go informing on me to your boyfriend; if Harris knows about the shuttle, it's the same thing as Jala knowing about the shuttle."

He didn't trust her to keep secrets from Harris for long. Kaden was probably alright, and he knew Kirby would keep her mouth shut. Misty would go along with whatever Kaden told her; she was such a follower. So, he really only had to worry about mousy, scared-of-her-own-shadow Stria.

"He's not my boyfriend," protested Stria weakly. She thought they'd done a better job of keeping up a professional front, but obviously everyone else had seen right through it. Had Jala noticed, too? She was bound to give Harris an earful if so. Maybe she'd even ban him from meeting with Stria. Would he obey his commanding officer if she did?

"That leaves Ivy, Zevon, Kaden, Misty, Ora, and Stria. And you, Drake," Kirby added, sensing Stria's discomfort and gallantly changing the subject again.

"Don't forget Reid," put in Kaden.

"Oh right, Dr. Everly. Well, that's eight people for a six-person shuttle. Better draw straws, I guess," Kirby added with unnecessary venom.

Maybe she's bitter about being forced to stay here for another year, thought Stria. *I know I would be. I **have** to be one of the six. But what about Harris? Will he want to leave, or will he stay on here, out of some misplaced duty to Jala?*

The rest of the table looked curiously at one another, wondering who'd be willing to take Drake up on his offer. No one volunteered, though it was clear several people were thinking it over.

"Swear to me on something that matters that none of you will tell Reid, Ivy, or Zevon about the shuttle. If they know, the Commander's bound to find out."

Drake didn't let anyone leave the table until they'd each sworn not to tell the others. Now he felt time really was running out. Maybe he'd have to finish things up tonight.

☆☆☆☆☆☆☆☆☆

Harris knocked on Jala's door well before breakfast. He wanted to get this over with.

"Look Jala," he began the second she opened the door. "I know we haven't had much time to sit and talk at dinner like we used to. I was hoping we could catch up a little bit this morning…"

He trailed off, remembering why he didn't like trying to rush into speech. It never turned out well and made him sound incredibly stupid. He thought Jala knew him well enough to understand, but he was beginning to wonder how well *he* knew *her*.

"I'm quite relieved to hear you say that, actually," she replied, waving him into her quarters, features softening a little.

"It has been a long time since we've been able to just **be**, if you understand my meaning. Now that I've been able to contact the shuttle and ensure they're following the proper coordinates, we should have more time together. I've missed our dinners, Harris," she continued, placing a warm hand against his arm.

"And I think," she added, withdrawing it quickly, "it might be best if you released Stria to the care of the other scientists. That's been another thing coming between us lately. I'd been meaning to bring it up earlier, but...well, we didn't really have the time before."

Seeing the dark look clouding his chiseled face, Jala rushed on before he could interrupt her.

"It's all my fault, I realize that—I never should have asked you to babysit her for so long. I should've known better. I put you at risk of entanglement and I apologize. But now that the danger's over and she seems to be doing alright, I think it's a good time for you to pull back. Whatever little emotions you've been entertaining for her are mere physical attraction, nothing more. I think when you've had a few days away from her, you'll see even that fade away."

Thanks to years of stone-faced practice, Shan remained oblivious to the storm raging inside her second-in-command.

Harris knew things between himself and Stria had developed quickly—after all, it had only been a few weeks—but he'd only felt this way once before, and he wasn't about to let Stria go just because it made Jala uncomfortable.

He also knew better than to get into an argument with Jala about his feelings. It would only create a rift between them, and right now, he needed her on his side. So there was really no point in discussing the matter further, because she would never change his mind about Stria, and he'd never be able to change hers.

For now, he allowed the insinuation that he didn't really care about Stria to pass. He'd have time to deal with that later. The most important thing today was asking Jala, "Why didn't you tell me the truth about what happened to the other two scientists, the ones who supposedly left right before Michael and Reid came?"

It was a good thing they were in the privacy of Jala's room because she froze for several minutes, her mouth opening and closing silently. She looked just like a fish gasping for breath.

"What—what—do you mean?" she finally said. "They **did** leave. You haven't seen them around the station these last two years, have you?" Harris knew this was her feeble attempt to lighten the mood, but it wasn't working on him.

"Jala, you don't have to lie to me. Stria and I discovered the bodies deep within Kraken Mare when we deployed the probe. There were **two** bodies in the sea, two bodies that could only be accounted for if they belonged to those two scientists. Obviously, they also succumbed to space sickness. Why else would they have run like that?"

"Space sickness," Jala muttered under breath, with a forced little laugh.

"Don't try to deny it. I can understand why you didn't tell the rest of the station—it's the same reason we didn't tell them about the other runners. But you could've told me! I'm not angry, I'm just disappointed that you didn't trust me. You don't have to keep this bottled up anymore, Jala. And you can trust me to keep it quiet."

"Can I?" she snapped. "Stria knows, doesn't she? Is that what you call keeping it quiet? That's why the two of you have been so cozy together, isn't it? Not because...yes, yes, I see now. Does *she* agree with your assessment that it was space sickness?"

Anger gave her voice an icy edge. "I suppose you'll need to brief me on what exactly you *have* told her."

She gave him a look of stern reprimand. Harris was completely taken aback. What did *she* have to be angry about? He was the one she'd been lying to for two years. Was it because of Stria? If it had been any other scientist who'd discovered the bodies, would Jala care quite so much? It left him floundering for something appropriate to say.

"I uh, told Stria that I knew the two bodies couldn't be Dr. Kamura or Dr. Thompson, because I'd been with you when they were incinerated."

He felt strange sharing this with Jala...for some reason, it felt like he was breaking a confidence. He also felt guilty for telling a scientist the secret of the runners when he promised he wouldn't. But there was something else at the back of his mind telling him not to say too much. He felt the need to protect Stria.

Shan's eyes bored into his.

"And what else did you tell her?" she demanded. "I know when you're holding out on me, Harris." She was fighting to keep up her calm demeanor, but Adley wasn't fooled, and it was making him very nervous.

"Umm, you see...I wasn't sure how much to tell her, because she was so frightened at first. She was afraid to even get near the Mare in the beginning, so I gave her the least possible amount of information to avoid scaring her."

"That doesn't quite answer my question. How much does Stria know about the runners, EXACTLY?"

Harris had rarely seen Jala this way. She was working herself into a rage. *Is she actually jealous? She never let on that she had any feelings toward me...but if she doesn't, then why does she care so much about Stria being involved in any of this?*

"I only told her that you'd led us to believe those two scientists had gotten on their shuttle back to Earth, so it was astonishing to me that...that you would've lied to me about what happened."

There, let her chew on that for a while.

Setting his jaw in a stern line, he refused to answer any more questions and stalked out of the Commander's quarters, convinced that she had more secrets up her sleeve.

☆☆☆☆☆☆☆☆☆

Jala sat on the bed in stunned silence, still fuming about her conversation with Harris.

To think I believed he could handle babysitting another scientist. Why, she's not even pretty! How he could have let himself get sucked into her confidence like that, I'll never know. Harris can't really love that girl; it's simply a silly, short-lived infatuation.

I should've told him my plans beforehand. That would have nipped any little romance in the bud. But maybe it's good I didn't share my plans with him after all. I may not have been able to count on him to follow through. Well, I'll just carry on by myself. After all, I took care of the shuttle on my own, didn't I?

Once Harris sees how well I've worked everything out for him, he'll come around. In another month or two, everything will be back on track.

✰✰✰✰✰✰✰✰✰

"Do you really think Drake was planning on running off in the shuttle without telling any of us first?" Misty asked Kaden as they wandered through the extensive greenhouse.

No wonder Drake and Kirby come here so often, Kaden thought. *It's like a whole other world back here.*

Aloud he said, "Oh, I don't know. He's pretty hard for me to read most of the time."

Kaden couldn't care less what Drake did or didn't do. He was only concerned with how this news might affect his relationship with Misty Lee.

Turning a serious face to her, he asked, "Misty, if you could leave right now, would you?" Kaden wasn't sure what answer he was hoping for, but he tensed up as if expecting the worst anyway.

"You know, I don't think I would. Being up here...I finally feel like I'm important! More important than I'd ever be back on Earth. There's something really comforting to me about seeing Saturn in the sky, too. And to be honest, I don't even mind the orange haze all the time. In fact, I've loved almost every minute of being here more than I ever thought I would!"

Kaden released his breath and relaxed. "I'm glad you feel that way. I like it up here, too. I don't see how anyone could get tired of the views and the crazy landscape and all the fascinating things to be discovered. I mean, we're blazing new trails up here, experiencing things that most people will never get the chance to. It's exhilarating!"

"So you wouldn't take the shuttle either?" She looked up at him curiously.

"No, I wouldn't. In fact, I wish I could stay longer."

"But you can! You could stay til the permanent crew leaves—I mean, if Drake leaves early, there will be an open seat for the trip back to Earth in four years."

"You wouldn't get tired of seeing me around for a few more years?" Kaden asked, suddenly nervous.

"Not at all," Misty sighed, already lost in his mahogany eyes.

22: Some Light Reading

Stria felt a little lost after the breakfast session broke up and everyone else went on to their assigned duties for the day. It didn't help that Harris had never appeared this morning.

She knew she should continue working on the formal write-up of their observations about the eel-creatures, but she couldn't seem to face the lab today. Instead, she found herself wandering around the station, not sure what she was looking for.

Her steps led her to the library, which she'd made a concerted effort to avoid ever since Michael's unfortunate accident. She felt a little guilty for walking inside, like she was disturbing the dead man's grave.

Taking a long look around now, it was clear there wasn't a huge variety of books to read, and nothing really appealed to her. She knew she was wasting time standing here, but she couldn't force her feet to leave.

Maybe one more look around before I go, she procrastinated. On the bottom shelf, a book title caught her eye. "The Habits of Aquatic Animals in Subzero Temperatures," nearly leapt out at her.

Hmm, that's a new one to me. And to think, I almost missed it— it's nearly hidden behind the bench.

She had to get down on her hands and knees in order to retrieve the book she wanted. She gave the title a slight tug, but the books were packed in so tightly that several of them piled onto the floor at once, revealing that Misty's little drones didn't clean the bottom shelves very often.

A glint of silver caused her to stop and examine the bottom of the shelf more closely. A small metal ring had been drilled into it.

Lifting up the ring, and feeling silly for hoping something exciting would happen, Stria startled herself when a small square section of the shelf came free.

Fishing her hand into the opening, her fingers landed on something smooth and square. She carefully pulled the object up through the shelf's false bottom, looking guiltily around as she did so.

Why, it's an old-fashioned, leather-bound journal! Whoever hid this sure went to a lot of trouble to keep it out of sight.

Stria turned the volume over—nothing on the outside. *Probably blank,* she thought. *But at least I can leaf through it before I put it back.*

Opening the slim journal, she read in perfectly-formed cursive handwriting:

"Confidential: Notes on the Psychological Study of Commander Jala Shan. Performed by Ulto Thompson, assigned to Titan Station Zero 2094. Informal, Supplementary Analysis Completed 2098."

Hmm, this is from nearly three years ago. Well, it probably wouldn't hurt anything to read it now, right?

Changing her mind about returning the book to its hiding place, Stria hurriedly replaced the bookshelf's false bottom, re-stacked the books, and snuck the journal to her room, glad that Commander Shan was keeping out of sight this morning.

✮✮✮✮✮✮✮✮✮

Stria locked herself in her room and checked the time—only an hour until lunch. She'd better hurry. She suddenly realized it might be a good idea to find a safe place to hide the journal. After all, someone had gone to a great deal of trouble to keep it out of sight, and she didn't want Misty stumbling across it when she cleaned the rooms.

After rejecting the bed, the closet, the chair, and the bathroom as too obvious, she finally decided to hide the slim volume in her uniform. If she kept her hand in one pocket, you couldn't tell it was there. With that settled, she gave herself up to the mysteries of Dr. Thompson's medical notes.

Alright, Jala, let's see what the good doctor had to say about you.

She felt a slight twinge of guilt. Should she really be reading a psychologist's private notes about someone she knew? In the end, her curiosity won out, and she began at the first entry, dated April 2095, almost five years ago.

Skimming Dr. Thompson's painstakingly written cursive notes, she didn't find much of interest. She decided to focus on the last few entries in the journal instead, and see if they could tell her anything about Dr. Kamura, space sickness, or what had really happened to the two scientists who'd somehow ended up in the Mare.

She flipped over to what looked like a promising date.

"November 2097. Commander Shan seems to be displaying some heretofore unknown signs of space sickness. She feels oddly possessive of Titan. Protective, I suppose, though in a very personal way. As if it were _her_ moon the rest of us were occupying. Fascinating. In her current state, she's of no harm to anyone (no one suffering from space sickness ever is), and is fully able to perform all the duties of her position, so I see no reason to make a formal report to Nasa at this time.

"December 2097. After further observation, I'm no longer confident Shan has space sickness. She continues to express healthy regard and care for her crew, but is increasingly antagonistic toward the scientists assigned to the station. While she isn't outright hostile toward them, she harbors a resentful attitude regarding their presence on her moon, though she feels no anger toward the crew, who are _also_ on her moon.

"January 2098. Shan's frustrations surrounding the scientists on Titan continue to manifest in unhealthy ways. When asked about the source of her frustration, she claims to be unhappy that they're sampling Titan's air, analyzing its chemical composition, and digging things up around the moon. She feels this is disrespectful, and has several times during our sessions voiced a wish to see the scientists leave. However, she was briefed on all of the activities Nasa wanted their scientists to perform before their arrival."

Stria skipped February and March, and would've skipped April, too, until she ran across a familiar name.

"April 2098. Harris Adley was the main topic of discussion during our session today, though Shan didn't realize she mentioned him so often. I think she's developing strong personal feelings for him. My sessions with Adley, however, reveal no such attachment on his part."

Here Stria paused. *I knew it! No wonder she's been so against our spending time together.*

So far, Dr. Thompson hadn't told her anything she hadn't already guessed, and she was starting to feel like maybe she shouldn't be diving into Jala's personal history.

But Stria wanted to at least read as far as the shuttle leaving and see if the writings could shed any light on what happened to the scientists. She skipped ahead a few more months, even though she only had a few minutes before lunch.

"August 2098. The shuttle arrived as scheduled yesterday, and took off as scheduled later that day, supposedly taking two scientists back to Earth. However, Dr. Kamura (according to Commander Shan) had a mental breakdown and insisted on leaving with the two departing scientists. That is medically impossible. Dr. Kamura was as mentally healthy as I am, and had no desire to leave the station early. There was nothing to indicate that he had developed space sickness, and would in no way have acted as Commander Shan described."

Now this is more like it, Stria thought.

"August 30, 2098. Assistant Commander Adley revealed to me that Dr. Kamura's body was found outside the station by two crew members. The theory Jala floated to Adley about why Dr. Kamura was outside the station alone, with gashes in his spacesuit, was once again, space sickness. As per my earlier notes, Dr. Kamura was in no way suffering from space sickness, and would not have acted in the irrational manner which Jala described. Due to the nature of his death, my professional opinion is that Dr. Kamura did not take his own life, either intentionally or accidentally. However, without additional physical evidence, I cannot make any accusations."

Stria reread the last two sentences. *If he didn't kill himself on accident, and he didn't kill himself on purpose, then that means...that means...he didn't kill himself at all! But then someone else must have...*

Stria thrust the book away from her. She wasn't sure she could keep reading. But what if Dr. Thompson had discovered who'd murdered Dr. Kamura?

She quickly scanned the next entry hoping for more information.

"September 2098. After today's session with Commander Shan, I am under the impression that she may have done something to one or both of the scientists before they left. She allegedly carried out her months-long plan to 'make the crew's life easier' at some point in August, but I have not seen any signs that this plan, whatever it may have been, was actually enacted. Shan is unwilling to openly discuss the shuttle's departure with me, or her feelings associated with it, and even became angry when I attempted to press further."

No luck. Well, she might as well finish up October and November while she was at it.

"October 2098. Commander Shan seems to think I am a threat to her in some way. She has made veiled references to my leaving (though I'm scheduled to remain on duty until end-of-mission just like the rest of the permanent crew). She's mentioned in several of our weekly sessions that psychology is a pseudo-science and serves no purpose. While she continues to meet with me on a regular basis, the sessions have now become tense, hostile, and counterproductive. Her outward behavior toward the rest of the crew remains pleasant and warm, and her behavior toward me when around others is also cordial."

"November 2098. I have taken it upon myself to do a formal psych eval of Commander Shan. The behaviors I have seen from her in our private sessions over the past two years have made me question the reliability of the pre-mission evaluations performed to determine a person's suitability for long-term space missions.

"After performing multiple informal evaluative techniques, and a few formal ones (for the entire crew, not only Shan), I am quite troubled, and question her fitness for command. She has been able to quite convincingly mask any and all negative feeling when it suits her.

"I have, on occasion, noted her uncanny ability to put on one persona in front of her crew and a completely different persona when she thinks she's alone. She seems to have an elevated view of herself as a mother/protector figure, and while remaining warm and loving toward her crew, I have begun to see signs that her ability to control her darker impulses is slipping.

"That being said, most of the crew have a positive relationship with Shan, and are seemingly unaware of her negative traits or characteristics. She has managed to keep her true feelings well hidden, and it is doubtful that anyone except a trained psychologist would be able to bring them to the surface.

"I am now firmly convinced that Shan caused some harm to come to the two departing scientists. I realize it seems far-fetched; however, the change in her manner since their 'departure' and her refusal to engage with me in meaningful discussion about it, leads me to believe that all is not as it seems. Unfortunately, there is only her word for what occurred. We know she lied about Dr. Kamura. It now appears she may have lied about other events related to the departing shuttle as well.

"In light of my professional evaluation of Jala Shan, and her deceptive behavior regarding the shuttle's departure, I feel that I must report to Nasa that Shan is unfit to retain command of the station. I will be recommending in my official report that Assistant Commander Adley be placed in charge of the station in her stead, and that Shan be sent back on the earliest possible shuttle in roughly two years. It is imperative for her mental health and the safety of the crew and scientists that she does not remain in command, or even on this station, for the full term of her assignment."

The lunch chime snapped Stria's thoughts back to the present. She did her best to walk calmly to the dining room while concealing the battle taking place in her mind. A few words and phrases kept coming back to her, circling around and around.

*There **is** space sickness, there is **no** space sickness; several people had it, only Jala had it; or did he say she didn't have it? Dr. Kamura was sane, and he didn't kill himself.*

Dr. Thompson wrote like a sane person; he didn't seem to have space sickness either.

If the two scientists who ended up in the Mare were completely healthy...then how did they get there? And what did it mean, that Dr. Thompson thought Jala was unfit for command?

He was going to report her, wasn't he? And then he died in a horrible, twisted-up way according to Harris. Did he ever make his report? Stria wondered, doing her best to calmly, steadily sit down at the dining table. Now she was worried about Harris being alone with Commander Shan.

Automatically, her hands went to her hair to braid it. She twisted several long sections into a rough, messy braid, undid it, and started again.

23: Final Repairs

Much to Drake's chagrin, Jala had stepped up her nightly rounds since Mike's death, making it much harder for him to sneak into the bay and complete his repairs on the shuttle.

The last time he tried sneaking over there at night, he'd run right into Jala and been forced to come up with a lame excuse for being out of his room after curfew, which he knew the Commander didn't buy. Worst of all, he'd been forced to scrap his repairs for the night and had to return to his room.

Continuing to attempt to sneak into the hangar after that was foolish, and he knew it, but he was almost finished and couldn't afford to quit now. *Just one more night,* he told himself, gathering the few tools he'd need for the final tune-ups.

He nervously checked the time. A little after one in the morning. If Jala were sticking to her normal routine, she should be back in her room by now.

It's probably safe, he thought anxiously, slowly opening his door. Not seeing anyone in the hallway, Drake began his quiet, careful creep to the hangar. He felt a little ridiculous, slinking behind every potted plant and waiting a few seconds before gliding silently to the next one.

It took an incredibly long time to get to the hangar that way, but he felt infinitely safer. He was confident (as always) that no one saw him slip inside the hangar and begin his night's work on the shuttle. *Only one more night,* he reminded himself between shaky breaths. *One more night.*

Taking a deep breath, he carefully slid the shuttle door open, looked quickly right and left, then crept silently inside. *So far, so good,* he thought grimly, thanking his lucky stars for the thousandth time that he'd never been caught in the act.

Sweat drifted along the concentration lines on his forehead, occasionally dropping to the floor below. *It won't be long now.* He only had to tweak a few wires, type in a couple of additional commands, and...*There, that should do it.*

He breathed a sigh of relief, finally allowing himself to wipe the pesky sweat from his forehead. His shoulders drooped, releasing the tension he'd been holding there from the moment he stepped into the darkened bay.

The final diagnostic was running now. If that went well, he could fly off this frozen moon tomorrow if he wanted. He was so absorbed in reading the real-time results of his test that he didn't see the quiet shadow fall across the floor.

His body suddenly tensed again, recognizing the sound of approaching footsteps before his brain did. Someone was heading right for the shuttle!

Still hoping the intruder would go away, he let the diagnostic finish running. *Just a few more seconds...*

Drake frantically tried to think of a way to stall for time.

"Hey, okay, you found me!" he began good naturedly, popping out of an access panel on the shuttle and jokingly putting his hands up.

Suddenly, a bright light was shining right in his face, blinding him.

"What's with that light? I've got my own, you know," he joked, but when the figure neither spoke nor removed the light, he began to worry for the first time. His mind went immediately to Mike's death.

What if my hare-brained idea was right, and it wasn't an accident after all?

"Listen, whoever you are, I'm going to need a few seconds to close up this panel and get my tools out of here, if you don't mind," he stalled, still holding his hands in the air.

"Make it quick," growled a garbled voice he didn't recognize.

A voice modulator? But why would anyone have one of those up here?

Slowly picking up the scattered tools, he noted that the diagnostic had completed its tasks and all systems were cleared. He went back to the access panel, and carefully activated a new feature he'd installed on the shuttle. He had thirty seconds to get the panel resealed and step away from the ship before his new defense system went online.

He felt confident the mysterious figure hadn't noticed—it was the smallest of buttons on the inner rim of the panel, and if you didn't know what you were looking for, you'd miss it entirely. Now no one could so much as touch the thing without getting blasted off their feet by the ship's brand-new security protocol system.

And he was the only one who could deactivate it. *Let Jala try to sabotage that!* He thought triumphantly. If he couldn't use the shuttle, then neither could anyone else.

Finally, I'll be able to get off this rock and there's nothing anyone can do to stop me.

When he turned to face the dark figure again, he was immediately struck with a heavy object, dropping to the floor without even knowing what hit him.

24: Disappointment

Kirby was in the middle of recalibrating the pressure on a minor pipeline inside the station, but she couldn't concentrate. Drake hadn't shown up for breakfast this morning, and he wasn't in the maintenance room after breakfast, either, leaving her to start on the day's jobs by herself.

So help me, if he got on that shuttle and took off last night when we were all asleep! And after he'd made it sound like he wanted us all to come, when the whole time he was planning on sneaking off without telling anyone. He's the worst kind of person—selfish and inconsiderate and conceited and...

Words failed her and she threw down her calibration tool in disgust. She needed to talk to someone.

Although it wouldn't be too long before lunch now, Kirby decided to pay a visit to Ivy and Zevon. There was no way she was going to leave them out of the loop, no matter what Drake wanted.

If she'd been hoping for a big reaction to her news that Drake had been secretly repairing the shuttle in the hangar for the past year, she didn't get it from the chefs. They were absorbed in getting lunch ready to serve, and frankly, pretty clearly absorbed in each other when they weren't plating food or making last minute adjustments to the seasonings.

"Well, it's not all that surprising, really, is it, Kirby?" Ivy asked with innocent eyes. "I mean, we know Drake likes to tinker around with things, and why not? No one ever said the shuttle was off-limits."

"It's not just that—he actually wants to fly away in it! And leave me here to take care of the lug nut's systems all by myself."

"Well, what do you think would've kept him here after next year's shuttle arrived, then, if he's already in such a hurry to go? It's just happened a year sooner, is all," Zevon added, with a quick look at Ivy.

Good riddance to the man, he thought. *The sooner Drake leaves, the better.*

Kirby couldn't help but feel that some sort of signal had passed quietly between them, and she'd been left in the dark.

"Fine, you don't care! I give up." Kirby stalked out of the kitchen and sat by herself at the last table. The only thing keeping her from attacking Drake right now in front of everyone in the dining room was the fact that he wasn't there.

Waylaying Commander Shan before she could steal away somewhere after lunch, Kirby didn't even try to keep her voice down when she brought up Drake's special hobby.

"I think you should know that Drake's been working on repairing the shuttle in the bay, and he's planning to take off in it pretty soon. Maybe even right now, since he hasn't managed to show up for lunch yet. And if you think I'm going to work on this station's systems all by myself, you're greatly mistaken."

Her light brown eyes flashed angrily as she looked at Jala, waiting for the other woman to act.

"That's impossible! I made sure...I'm sure the shuttle isn't operational," she exploded. This uncharacteristic outburst got the room's attention, and every eye was glued to her face, wondering what she'd do next.

Much to their collective disappointment, Jala recovered herself, saying, "I'll go talk to Drake about this," in a low voice, inwardly cursing her bad luck.

Stria was taking everything in with wide eyes—and she for one didn't miss the meaning behind Jala's words. It was amazing how a little light reading before lunch could change your perspective on things. She might not be a psychologist, but she'd been trained to detect patterns and anomalies in her work as an oceanographer, and she put those skills to good use. Now she was closely examining Jala's face, words, and gestures in minute detail.

Kirby, not about to be left behind, led the search to Drake's room, but he wasn't there. She knew he wasn't in the maintenance area, but they checked there, too, just in case. With a sinking feeling, Kirby suggested they check the hangar bay, worried the shuttle, and Drake, would be gone for good.

To her surprise, however, Jala insisted on talking to Drake inside the hangar alone.

"And from this point forward," Shan added, as if the thought had just occurred to her, "the hangar will be coded to a key only I and Assistant Commander Adley have, so one of us will have to accompany anyone who wants to use the bay for any purpose from now on."

Kirby stood there awkwardly, watching the Commander walk through the bay door. She decided to stay put until Shan came back out. *Drake's not going to get away with this!* She knew it was petty, but she was highly disappointed she couldn't be there to see Drake get raked over the coals.

✩✩✩✩✩✩✩✩✩

Reid was dismayed by the animalistic display of emotions playing out all around him at lunch. *What a mess they are,* he thought unkindly, and went back to daydreaming about being the savior of the human race with his bacteriological research. *If only they knew who was walking among them, they'd behave themselves better.*

✩✩✩✩✩✩✩✩✩

Zevon and Ivy, meanwhile, were actually having a private celebration in the kitchen over Drake's imminent departure. Ivy couldn't believe her good fortune—she'd finally be rid of Drake and could enjoy a full year of peace on the station before heading back to Earth with Zevon.

It was the best news she'd received in a long time.

25: Disruptions

Harris finally emerged from his room after lunch. He'd been thinking again about Jala's lies; and who'd been told what. What if she'd been lying to him from the beginning?

He was struggling to make sense of it all and doing a terrible job of it. He needed Stria's clear mind to help him put the pieces together in the right way.

He was on his way to her room when the sight of Kirby pacing outside the bay door stopped him in his tracks.

"What are you doing?" he asked in bewilderment, since the engineer could easily enter the bay anytime she wanted.

"Shan locked me out of the hangar, and I'm pretty sure she's letting Drake have it for fixing up the shuttle without telling anyone," she gleefully replied.

"I'd love to be in there to hear what she's saying," Kirby hinted, though Assistant Commander Adley didn't bite.

"You must be joking," he choked, "and it's not very funny."

"No joke, see for yourself," she challenged, pointing to the access panel.

Before he could unlock the door, however, Stria rushed over to him, gasping for breath.

"Harris," she urgently whispered, clutching the Assistant Commander's hand, "I have to talk to you."

Kirby raised her eyebrows suggestively as Harris reluctantly followed Stria to her room.

"I should really be helping Jala get this situation with Drake under control," he pleaded. "Besides, if I keep sneaking off to your room like this, the rest of the station's going to start making up their own ideas about why we're spending so much time alone together," Harris muttered self-consciously.

"Oh, it's too late for that, I'm afraid. Drake already thinks you're my boyfriend, and I gather the rest of the crew does, too."

"He does? I had no idea Drake paid much attention to anything but himself." He looked searchingly into Stria's eyes. "And how do you feel about that?"

"About them thinking you're my boyfriend or about you actually being my boyfriend?"

"Both. Either. I don't know." The confused look on his face intensified, and he could feel a headache slowly coming on.

Back in her room now, Stria took Harris' hand in hers and pulled him closer. He looked deeply into her eyes. It felt so good to be close to her that he wrapped his arms around her waist without thinking. *She has no idea how beautiful she is.*

He pulled her in for a kiss when she whispered gently but firmly, "I think we should come back to this another time, don't you?"

She was throwing cold water all over his fantasies before they could even get started. He allowed himself one last longing gaze into those beautiful blue eyes of hers before getting down to business.

"All right," he said, pulling the armchair over to the bed and sitting down, "what did you need to talk to me about?"

"Harris, I'm worried about you. I don't think it's safe for you to be alone with Jala right now. I mean, if only you'd heard what she said about the shuttle at lunch!"

"I'm sure she was just as surprised by the news as I was," Harris sighed. "After all, it wasn't Drake's place to work on it in secret."

"But that's not what she seemed so upset about. She said she thought she'd made sure it wasn't operational. Don't you see? She was positive the ship wouldn't be able to get off Titan. And she was shocked to find out that Drake had been able to make it work again!"

"Why would she care whether that shuttle works or not?" he asked, incredulous. Was Stria getting jealous now? He would never understand women.

"Oh, I don't know—but she does. And I'd be willing to bet it has something to do with this."

Triumphantly producing Dr. Thompson's journal, she placed it in one of Harris' large hands.

"This contains Dr. Thompson's psychology notes on Commander Shan," she added. "Not that I was trying to pry into her personal life or anything, but there are some entries around the time the scientists disappeared, and..." She dropped her eyes under Harris' disapproving gaze.

"Stria, what does any of this have to do with what's been happening lately? These notes are several years old. Do you really hate Jala so much that you'd stoop to this?"

"But Harris, he thought Dr. Kamura was murdered!"

His neck whipped around like he'd been slapped. "What?"

"Look, right here—this entry dated August 30th—there!"

Harris dutifully read the passage she pointed out to him, then turned dark, puzzled eyes toward her. "How did you find this?"

"It was a complete accident—I was in the library and when I tried pulling out a book I wanted, all the other books tumbled out with it, and then I saw a metal ring on the bottom of the shelf. When I grabbed the ring, the entire bottom section of the bookcase came up with it. The journal was in there."

"I can't believe it, after all this time...it's like he's come back from the dead."

A brief image of the psychologist's dead face popped into his head. Closing his eyes, he forced the image away.

"I realize this might be hard to process...I'm still working my way through it, too. But there's more, AND it gets worse. At least, if I'm understanding things right, it does. And I think you should read it for yourself."

Perching on the arm of Harris' chair, she wrapped herself around him, silently preparing him for the blow to come. If it had been rough reading for Stria, how much tougher would it be on Harris to realize that his beloved Commander had been slowly losing her mind?

✫✫✫✫✫✫✫✫✫

Now to deal with that shuttle once and for all. How Drake could take it into his head to do something so foolish, Jala thought, heading inside the hangar after Kirby's unpleasant revelation.

Anyone could take it into their heads to try and fly this thing out of here! But, just to be sure...

She removed a hydraulic tool from one of the nearby workbenches and took aim at the shuttle's nose. Much to her surprise, she was jolted backward with such force that she was thrown to the floor five feet away from the ship.

What has Drake done? Jala wondered in frustration. *I had no idea it was even possible to do this to a ship!*

In spite of herself, she had to admit that she was impressed with Drake's skills. *I always knew he was a good engineer—but I never realized how good.*

Determined to break down the shuttle's defense system, she tried again, with something a little less powerful this time, just in case the force of the blast had been the hydraulic's fault.

Picking up a plain, simple hammer, she gave the nose a good whack. And was again lifted off her feet and thrown back against the floor.

Not one to give up easily, Jala tried again and again. Each time, the shuttle resisted her efforts to disable it.

Infuriated now, Jala thought, *If Drake thinks a simple deflection system will stop me, he's sadly mistaken. I will find a way to fix this. After all, I've always managed to fix everything else.*

26: Insinuations

Harris was at a loss for words. That in itself wasn't too surprising, since it happened whenever he was alone with Stria for too long, but this was for an entirely different reason.

He didn't like what he'd been reading, and stopped several times to gather his thoughts and work through the implications with Stria.

Everything he thought he knew about space sickness, and Jala, and the runners, was crashing down around him. The room was starting to spin, and he had to grip Stria's hand tightly to make it stop.

The entries abruptly ended after November 30, 2098, and the last entry didn't contain much. It indicated that Dr. Thompson had informed Jala he was going to file a report with NASA outlining his opinion that she was no longer fit for command.

"That would have been around the time we found Dr. Thompson's body...December 1st or November 30th—right around then."

"Do you think Jala had something to do with his death? If he was going to report her, and she was aware of it..."

"She'd never do anything like that! I've known her for seven years. She couldn't kill anyone. I'm sure of it."

"She's really proud of this station, you know," Stria began, seemingly off-topic. "And of her role as Commander. If anyone threatened to take that away from her... You can at least admit that the timing of his death seems a *little* suspicious, can't you? And that it would be devastating for her to lose command of this station?"

Harris had to confess that Jala lived for the station. She was born to command, and believed that Fate had guided her to Titan.

Poor Harris, he looks like a wounded animal. He genuinely looked up to that woman. I only hope I'm not pushing him too far.

"It would be sort of convenient, wouldn't it," she boldly continued, "to casually say another scientist contracted space sickness, since she'd already said it before? This may seem like a leap, but we know she lied about the two scientists, so what if she had something to do with their deaths, too? And Dr. Kamura?"

That roused Harris from his confused stupor. He'd finally seen where she was going with all of this nonsense and he didn't like it. He jumped up, accidentally knocking Stria off the chair and onto the floor.

"That's absolutely insane!" he bellowed. "You can't actually be serious, Stria. You've simply made the whole thing up from your overworked imagination because you read something that scared you!"

He decided not to stick around and hear any more crazy conspiracy theories about his Commander, rushing out the door and back toward the hangar, where he should've been all along.

*Of all the cruel things to do to another person's character. To sit there and calmly say they're a murderer! And not just any murderer, but a serial killer! Maybe I **have** been wrong to let my feelings for Stria run away with me. I'll have to be more careful in future. Jala was right. As usual.*

She's the best commander I've ever had, and she cares about the crew like they're her own children.

That sounded slightly familiar, and Harris realized with a start that's exactly how Dr. Thompson had described her, too. Only **he** thought she was crazy.

Still fuming, Harris tapped in the new security code only he and Jala had access to.

*Stria's completely off-base; I know it. And how can I be sure that Dr. Thompson's writings weren't the ravings of a madman who'd fallen under the spell of space sickness? Maybe **he** was the paranoid one, not Jala.*

That's what Harris needed to believe, so he did.

Until he saw Drake's body lying in a heap on the hangar floor, waiting for the incinerator.

Almost immediately, an arc of blue-white light flashed from the shuttle and tossed someone to the ground. He ran closer and realized it was Jala.

"Are you alright?" he shouted.

"No, I'm not," Jala said, struggling a little to get to her feet.

"Wait, let me help you!" Harris shouted, rushing anxiously to her side. She was trembling uncontrollably.

"Lean against me until the tremors pass. What's going on out here? It looks like a full-on combat zone. And what on Earth happened to Drake?"

"I don't suppose you were aware that Drake repaired this shuttle right under our noses," Jala began weakly, panting for breath.

"He prepped it for flight, and also enacted some kind of security protocol on this shuttle to keep everyone else out. Apparently, he snuck in here after I made my nightly rounds—for at least the past year, and who knows how much longer! He'd even planned on flying himself out of here before end-of-mission!"

She was nearly hyperventilating now from the effort to speak, and Harris had her sit down on the floor, taking slow, deep breaths before he was willing to allow her to continue.

After a minute or two, she added, wheezing, "I can only assume the security protocol failed, and he was unable to re-enter the ship. I found him like this when I came in here this afternoon."

"So he really did manage to do it? I hoped it was something he'd made up to impress the rest of the crew."

"Not a story, unfortunately," Shan affirmed. "I've tried to breach the system multiple times, and I can't shut it down. It's my fault, you know," she continued, looking sadly at Harris.

"My nightly patrols were supposed to keep things like this from happening."

Disgusted with herself, she slammed her right fist into her left palm, wincing a little at the pain. That system of Drake's had taken more out of her than she'd thought.

Carefully helping her back up, Harris noted that she was limping, and her uniform had been singed in several places. He hated seeing her like this—beaten down, defeated, feeling like she'd failed in her duty to protect the civilians on the station.

He led her to the workbench and ordered her to rest a minute while he examined Drake's prone form. His uniform had been singed too, just like Jala's.

On further inspection, Harris discovered a small pool of blood seeping from the back of Drake's head, and wondered, not for the first time, if Jala had told him the whole truth.

✮✮✮✮✮✮✮✮✮

A small crowd was gathering outside the bay doors, waiting to see what Jala would have to say about Drake's deception, and whether he'd still be allowed to fly off the moon early or not.

Kirby was happier than she'd been in weeks, relishing in the thought that Drake would finally get his comeuppance at Jala's hands.

This is going to be so delicious! As the bay doors began to slowly open, she realized it wouldn't be long now.

27: Confession

Harris and Commander Shan made their slow, tedious way into the station, and ordered everyone to the dining room for a quick debrief. It wasn't going to be pleasant, but he knew that telling everyone about Drake's death was the right thing to do.

But if Stria attempted to use this meeting as an excuse to accuse Jala of mass murder, Harris wouldn't hesitate to put a stop to it.

He led Jala carefully to her room, so she could freshen up a bit before the difficult discussion that was about to take place.

The rest of the station, minus Drake, was already waiting for them in the dining room when they arrived. The other members of the permanent crew, much like Harris, were shocked to see the condition Commander Shan was in.

While she'd smoothed her hair back into a tight bun, it was clear she wasn't well. She still had a very visible limp, and hadn't let go of Harris' arm since they'd entered the dining room.

Scanning the expectant faces, Harris noted that for some strange reason, Reid had a projection device and a microscope with him, and seemed quite unhappy to be there. *Join the club, Reid. Join the club.*

Harris cleared his throat, uncharacteristically nervous. He could tell they were getting a little restless, wondering why they'd been summoned here in the middle of the afternoon. Stria caught his eye and nodded encouragingly. *You can do this*, her warm smile assured him.

"So you're probably all wondering why we gathered you here this afternoon," he began, taking a deep breath as he spoke. "I know it's early and most of you have work to do around the station or in the labs, so I appreciate your willingness to sacrifice your time."

He scanned the curious faces once more, stalling for time, and took another hopeful glance at Stria. *It's now or never. Deep breath and...*

"We...made an unfortunate discovery this afternoon," Harris continued, nodding toward Jala as he spoke. "It seems that Drake, while doing unapproved repair work to the shuttle, had a tragic accident."

Jala looked as if she might drop to the floor, and Harris gripped her arm tightly.

"Another **accident**?" Kirby moaned before slumping forward in her seat. Kaden leapt over to her in time to keep her from hitting the floor, and Zevon helped him prop her up against a chair.

A confused chorus of voices demanded answers to a flood of

questions simultaneously.

"How did it happen?"

"When did he die?"

"How do you know it was an accident?"

"Is this related to what happened to Michael?"

Several pairs of startled, fearful eyes turned toward Harris, and he realized he had a new problem on his hands. If fear got a hold of the group, there's no telling what could happen.

He looked over to Jala for help, but she was barely holding herself upright. Those blasts from the shuttle defense system that Drake rigged up must have hurt her far more than she'd let on.

"Jala, you're not looking very well. Would you like to sit down?"

She didn't protest, so he gently led her to the nearest chair and ordered Ivy to bring her something to drink.

It looked like Kirby was coming around again, and Zevon took it upon himself to bring drinks and appetizers out to the whole group. He was thankful Ivy'd had the foresight to insist on always keeping a few "extras" on hand just in case the need arose.

Seeing everyone relax a bit with some food and drink in them, Harris tried to explain the unexplainable.

Not sure the best place to really begin, Harris started at the end, with Drake. "I personally witnessed the power of Drake's security system on Jala this afternoon. She was trying to access the shuttle, and it threw her several feet into the air. I can easily imagine the same thing happening to Drake."

Stria shook her head, and gave Harris a cynical look. He knew what *she* thought happened, and as much as he didn't want to believe it himself, he was having a hard time making sense of Jala's latest story.

"But," stated Ora firmly, "if Drake set up the defense system, why wasn't he able to disarm it? It doesn't seem likely to me that he would've been incapacitated by his own system."

That was a tough question to answer, and Harris didn't know what to say.

Stria did, however. "I agree, Ora," she began defiantly, taking her courage in both hands. "I think you'll find that there are several mysterious deaths the Commander may have been involved in. Take Dr. Kamura, for instance." *There, that'll get things rolling in the right direction,* Stria thought victoriously.

"But I thought he had space sickness!" Misty chimed in, really confused about what was going on now. First, he'd fled on a shuttle. Then he'd died on Titan. And now Stria was implying that Commander Shan had something to do with his death?

Harris looked over at his Commander, but she was unnaturally pale and statue-still, staring off into the distance, seemingly unaware of the chaos unfolding around her.

No one wanted to believe what Stria was implying, and yet...couldn't they imagine it, just a little bit? Everyone was talking over everyone else, except for Stria, who had a pretty concrete idea of what she believed happened, and Reid, who looked like he just wanted to be removed from it all.

"Stop!" Harris shouted in desperation, unsure if his voice would be heard over all the others. A momentary hush settled over the room.

"Working yourselves into a panic isn't going to do anyone any good," Harris reprimanded. "Now, I've already shared with you everything I know about Drake's death. There are a few other questions I can answer, and many more that I can't. For instance, if any of you were thinking about using the repaired shuttle, you should know that the hangar has been coded to a key that only Jala and I have. And, from what I just witnessed, Drake rigged it so that even if you did get into the hangar, you'd never be able to get into the shuttle, let alone touch it, without him. So I certainly hope no one's thinking of attempting to fly off Titan."

That seemed to take the wind out of their sails, so at least for now, a mutiny had been avoided. But for how long, Harris couldn't be sure. He'd hoped Jala would add her two cents worth about Drake, but she remained silent, watching the proceedings without emotion.

"Now, let me address Dr. Kamura's death," Harris sighed, frustrated that Misty, at least, seemed to know more than she should, and worried that Stria had told her. How many others knew the truth, he wasn't sure, but he wanted to set the record straight in front of all of them, just in case. (Without feeding into Stria's unfounded presumptions of Jala's murderous guilt, of course.)

While Stria hoped he'd directly accuse Jala of Dr. Thompson's death, she realized there were plenty of other ways to squeeze a confession out of the Commander, and she wasn't above trying a few of them in the relative safety of the group if Harris wouldn't.

For now, she waited patiently for him to present things in his own way and his own time.

Jala seemed to be in her own world as Harris spoke, barely acknowledging the presence of the others, and only looking at Harris once in a while.

There were so many layers to the deception that had to be unpeeled. That was the hardest thing for Stria to come to terms with. Layer one was the lie about Dr. Kamura's disappearance that a few people continued to believe in spite of what Kirby and Drake had told them.

Layer two was the story Jala'd made up for Kirby and Drake's benefit about how Dr. Kamura got outside the station. (Stria believed that was a lie, too, after reading Dr. Thompson's journal entries.)

Layer three was the lie about the two scientists—the bodies she and Harris had uncovered drifting in the Mare.

Layer four was the death of Dr. Thompson. All wrapped up in the convenient blanket of space sickness and centered on one person's word for everything—Jala. How Harris could continue to give her the benefit of the doubt after all this was the real mystery to Stria.

As Harris walked back all the lies the crew had been told, Stria continued to pay special attention to Commander Shan. She stirred a few times during his recitation, and once or twice looked like she was going to contradict him over some little detail, but she never interrupted and let Harris tell the entire story himself.

At last, he finally shared everything with the crew that he'd either personally seen or been told by Jala.

"Now," he finished, exhaustion creeping into his voice, "I've told you everything I know, but Jala can probably answer more of your questions than I can. If you're feeling up to it, Commander, would you please...?"

He knew the group would have questions that only she could answer, and he hoped she was in a good enough mental state to address them.

Commander Jala Shan stood up stoically. She was still a little wobbly from going ten rounds with the defense shield in the hangar, but she seemed well enough to speak, though Harris noticed with a jolt that she appeared years older than she had just a few hours ago.

Well, she **had** told a great number of lies to the crew, and it was finally catching up to her.

"Yes, Harris," she replied in an odd monotone, looking out at the crowd—her crew, people who'd been like family to her for six years.

"I think it's finally time I told our wonderful, hard-working crew the truth. Understand that what I've done, I've done to protect you all. And to preserve our way of life on the station. The truth..." she was lost in thought for a second, then seemed to make up her mind.

"The truth is, next year's shuttle isn't coming."

"What?" Stunned, Harris whispered, "But you said that you'd made contact and corrected their flight path?"

The dining room was so silent, it was as if he'd shouted the question.

"I did correct their flight path," Jala said complacently. "I sent the shuttle away from here."

Kirby's confusion was quickly replaced by fury as she realized what Jala had done.

"Where...did...you...send...that...ship?" Kirby demanded, hurling each word like a bullet.

"Oh, somewhere out into deep space—they'll continue on that path until their ship runs out of fuel, and then they'll drift forever and ever, in eternal sleep. Really, it's a most peaceful way to die," Shan added matter-of-factly.

She spoke with the same amount of emotion she'd use when teaching someone how to operate a rover.

"My sister is on that ship! You've sentenced her to die!!" Kirby screamed at the Commander, jumping up so fast, Kaden didn't have time to hold her back. If it hadn't been for Zevon's lightning reflexes, she would have landed a punch square on the Commander's jaw. She was within inches of Jala's face when Zevon grabbed her right arm and held it tight.

Jala raised her eyebrows in consternation, but otherwise, had no response.

"This won't help your sister, Kirby," Zevon said gently. She slumped against him as the adrenaline subsided, and let him guide her back to her seat.

"But why?" Harris demanded, resuming as if nothing had happened. "How could you do something like that? We trusted you! *I* trusted you!!" *How many times has Jala lied to me over the years? Can I trust what she's telling us now?*

"More of the truth?" Jala looked emptily around the room once more. She'd become strangely detached, and most of those watching barely recognized the woman they all thought they knew so well.

"To be honest, I couldn't stand the thought of one more group of smug, meddling scientists coming up here and looking down their noses at the rest of us because they have advanced degrees and we don't. And to watch them cutting and chopping and dissecting this perfect, pristine world. Did they learn nothing from Earth? They'll end up ruining this moon and moving on to the next to extract whatever they want from it and then when that's ruined, too, they'll go on to the next and the next and the next.

"I wasn't going to simply sit back and watch them do that to Titan," Shan continued with more emotion than she'd shown so far.

Something clicked in Harris' brain. He looked over at Stria, who seemed to be taking it all in stride. She hadn't been surprised because she'd believed the worst about Jala from reading Dr. Thompson's journal. *He knew something like this would happen, didn't he? That's why he thought Jala was unfit for command.* The mixed-up puzzle pieces were starting to form a clear pattern in Harris' mind, but he didn't like the picture that was emerging.

"We needed that shuttle to get home!" Reid was shaking with quiet fury. "You've doomed us all to live up here permanently!" *The futility of it all.* He'd made one of the greatest scientific breakthroughs in human history, and he would be forever trapped up here, unable to enjoy the fruits of his very productive labor.

"But I thought there were supposed to be more shuttles on the way—I mean, someone has to come to pick up me, Ora, and Stria in 2103, right?" Kaden, who'd been quietly taking everything in up to this point, had to believe that Reid was mistaken.

"Tell us he's wrong, Adley. There's no way the last shuttle that was ever going to come here is the one that's pinging around the outer edges of the Universe somewhere! Sorry, Kirby," he added as an aside, suddenly remembering that her sister was pinging around the Universe for eternity, too.

"You're partly right, Kaden. The original plan was to send multiple shuttles," Harris said wearily, worn down by the realization that Jala's meddling would force them all to stay on Titan a lot longer than originally planned.

"NASA realized it was too costly and not very efficient to send shuttle after shuttle to one outpost, so they made a course correction. They rerouted the shuttle that would have arrived here in 2107 to take us all home to another colony—one of the moons of Neptune, I think. They upgraded the shuttle that's now lost to contain two detachable mini-shuttles—one for Reid and..."

He was going to say Michael but remembered he was dead.

"...for Reid to take home next year, and one to take Ora, Kaden, and Stria back to Earth in 2103. The main shuttle was supposed to remain docked in the bay and take the rest of us home in 2107. So, yes, Reid is technically correct, though we're not going to be here forever, of course. Once we explain to NASA what happened, they'll requisition another shuttle, equip it for the journey here and back, and send it on its way to us."

"But how long will that take?" Ivy asked. It was devastating—to be so close to her dreams only to have them yanked away from her.

Harris tried to keep his emotions in check—as the station's Second-in-Command, it was up to him (now that Jala was clearly unfit) to keep everything under control and make sure the others remained calm.

"It could take up to two years for them to find, prepare, and send another ship here, and then, of course, another seven years to make it to Titan, so all-in-all, it only puts the crew two or three years behind when we were originally scheduled to leave," he said as hopefully as possible.

"Why should NASA send another ship out here?" Jala suddenly interrupted. "They've realized by now that I can disrupt a ship's navigation systems once it gets within a year of Titan. You don't really think they'd risk losing a second precious shuttle to the vastness of the universe, do you? Or the additional lives?" she added almost as an afterthought. "And besides, even if they did send a second ship, I wouldn't let them come anywhere near Titan."

"Of course they'll send more ships up here. Crew after crew after crew," Stria chimed in, outrage giving her a boldness she rarely displayed.

"They'll have to—after all, Titan's the only other place in the Universe with life on it—right now! Not a million years in the past, but living and breathing now. They'll have to come; there's no way they could resist sending more groups up here to take specimens and transport them to Earth. I know I've only seen two of the eel-creatures, but that was based on two weeks' worth of mapping only part of one of the mares. I'm sure there are more. And other creatures we haven't even discovered yet!"

"Who said NASA knows there's life up here?" Commander Shan smirked, with an iciness rivaling that of Titan itself.

I knew I shouldn't have come here, Stria fretted. *I knew it. And now it really is too late...*

"How can they not know?" Reid spluttered in disbelief. "I've been giving you the results of the research on my beautiful little bacteria for nearly two years now!"

Harris stared in astonishment. He knew how. All communications with NASA went through Jala. "You never sent those reports, did you?"

"Of course not! The last thing I wanted was more scientists traipsing around up here, destroying my precious moon, mucking up the routine on this station, and interfering with the lives of my crew."

Here she paused for a moment to look Stria up and down. The other woman shivered.

"Well, I couldn't stop everyone," Jala continued coldly, "but I could stop a few. Now we can live up here for as long as we want, and we won't have to deal with any more newbies getting in the way of things. I don't suppose I can do anything about those of you who are here now, unfortunately, though Michael was a good start," she continued, undisturbed by the terror she saw slowly spreading across her subordinates' faces.

"I'd created a lovely story about what happened to him and everything."

Harris couldn't comprehend that this was the same Jala who'd been his commander for all these years. The compassionate, motherly figure who'd held the crew together from the beginning, making sure everyone felt safe and cared for on her watch.

What sane person would sentence an innocent group of people to die in space because their presence might be inconvenient or annoying? This is our job, for crying out loud—hosting groups of scientists conducting experiments.

This was what we signed up for. And Jala decided she wasn't going to do it anymore. Only instead of resigning, taking the next shuttle home, and forfeiting command, she's become—something less than human. Alien. Unable to feel for her own species anymore.

"You killed them all, didn't you?" Harris surmised gloomily. "Dr. Thompson, and Dr. Kamura, and those two scientists whose bodies Stria and I discovered in Kraken Mare. Why did you do it?"

He was a broken man, desperate for any answer at all, clinging to a last shred of hope that he was wrong. That she'd face him and say she'd had nothing to do with any of it. That she'd been playing the worst kind of joke on him, on all of them, and none of it was true after all.

Much to his dismay, she didn't deny it. "Yes, I did," Jala replied calmly.

"As to why, well, I had to get rid of Dr. Thompson, of course," she explained with indifference. "He was going to comm NASA and tell them I wasn't fit for command. And I wasn't going to give up my station for anyone. So, I asked him to join me in the hangar one night, and hit him over the head when he was examining some wires I'd cut. Once I was suited up to leave the station, I dragged him outside the bay doors, came back in, put the tool back, and sanitized myself in the refining room. How was I supposed to know he was still alive when I tossed him outside? He tried to crawl toward the doors, but the cold quickly took care of that. I think he had about three or four seconds to react before he was dead."

"I knew it!" Stria nearly shouted, then felt bad for being triumphant about something so gruesome.

"Good for you," Jala said, amused. "If I may proceed? I also had to kill Dr. Kamura. Personally, I liked the man, and I was sorry I had to do it. But, you see, I couldn't have him contradicting me on death certificates, now could I? I told him there was something urgent we needed to examine outside the station and the fool believed me! I brought my knife and was easily able to take him by surprise. He never even saw it coming. Child's play, really. Then I moved his body to where Kirby and Drake found him later, to help authenticate my story about space sickness."

Kirby snorted in disgust. "And you made Drake and me keep your dirty little secret for two years?! All for some stupid lie! I've been reliving the moment we found him every day for the past two years. Because of you!" And now her sister was going to die because of Jala, too. She slammed her fist on the table, making Misty and Stria jump.

Misty just shook her head in sorrow. She'd believed in Jala; had felt close to her, even. This, all of this, was unforgivable.

"So why didn't you let the two scientists leave in the first place?" Ora asked, unwillingly admiring Jala's ability to keep so many lies straight for so long.

"And let them go back to Earth and fill people's ears with tales of how enchanting and exciting life on Titan is? Of the magical discoveries waiting to be uncovered on this virgin land? For them to go back and gather more experimenters and pokers and prodders to come up here and rip Titan apart? It would be the Conquistadors all over again. Never!"

Harris realized as he studied her unnaturally bright eyes and feverish features that Jala had gone past the point of no return. In fact, he thought she'd have no qualms about trying to kill the remaining scientists, even though there'd be no more stories about space sickness or accidents. Even though everyone would know she'd done it.

She'd kill now because she wanted to, because she was good at it, and because she'd been able to get away with it for so long. Even though they'd all know who was responsible, he honestly didn't believe that would prevent Jala from attempting to remove the scientists who were left on the station.

And then he realized what everyone else had probably already figured out by now.

"You killed Drake, too, didn't you?" That was six deaths at her hands.

Jala couldn't help gloating just a little. "And you were so willing to believe he'd been hurt by own defense system!" she laughed mockingly.

Harris felt sick to his stomach. The woman he'd known for so many years was gone, and he was left staring into the face of a complete stranger.

Hearing first Harris, and then Jala, reveal how many of the things they'd taken for granted on this station weren't even true had drained the crew and scientists of all emotion. No one even had the energy to move from their seats.

A few times someone would try to say something, but words wouldn't come, and they'd go back to looking at one another mutely, barely able to muster the effort necessary to do even that.

28: Sentence

I t was Kirby who finally broke the uncomfortable silence. "I think I could disable the security system Drake set up on the shuttle, but I'd need to have access to his room to look over his schematics."

"You mean there's a chance we could still use it to get off the station?" Stria asked, trying not to show her excitement.

"Yes, if enough of us are willing to stay behind and wait for the replacement shuttle from NASA."

"Well, how many of us are there who'd want to leave?" Ora asked, her practical mind cutting to the heart of the matter.

Kaden was doing the math now. He and Misty, Ivy and Zevon, Harris and Stria, Ora, Reid, Mich—no, not Michael. He was at eight already. And that wasn't including Kirby and Jala—though he wasn't sure if she'd willingly leave Titan or not.

"There are ten of us, and Drake said only six people could fit."

"Aren't you forgetting something?" Zevon asked, his deep voice rumbling through the crowd. He jerked his head toward where Jala was still standing. She'd made no effort to move during the intervening silences and even now, didn't seem interested in trying to escape. She merely stood there, waiting like a wary animal, sizing up its opponents.

After some debate, which Jala surely heard, it was decided that she should be locked in her room. Kirby re-programmed the door so the Commander couldn't get out unless someone else opened it from the outside.

"Harris," Jala begged, "you know I can't stay cooped up in my room like this, locked away from the rest of the station. I'll go crazy in here."

Harris didn't think she was being ironic. He understood how hard this was for her, to feel caged, to lose the respect and trust of her crew. He knew all of this on an objective level, but it didn't move him. Sensing this, she tried someone else.

"Misty—you've always been the compassionate one on the station...you know I can't be left in here like a zoo animal."

It was extremely difficult for Misty to see the Commander this way. She'd been a surrogate mother to her for so many years. Tears were streaming down her face as Kaden pulled her away before she could respond to Jala's wild-eyed plea. He wasn't about to let that evil woman get away with any more lies.

Kirby dashed off to Drake's room once the Commander was safely locked in her quarters to begin the tedious process of deactivating the defense mechanism he'd installed. After several hours, she finally found something she thought could work.

Harris unlocked the hangar, then nervously watched as Kirby typed in a series of commands. He held his breath when she finally placed her hands against the shuttle's hull and let it out in a big sigh when nothing happened.

Kirby'd done it, and now they'd be going home.

29: Escape

It felt a little anticlimactic, but Ivy and Zevon knew how much the station's inhabitants needed their strength, and felt the best way they could help everyone now was to feed them. It was almost time for dinner, anyway, so they went back to work in the kitchen, while the others talked together in hushed voices in the dining room until dinner was ready.

It was silly, they realized, but no one wanted Commander Shan to overhear what they were saying, even though she was safely locked away in her soundproof room.

During dinner, talk centered around who should leave now and who should remain on the station until the replacement shuttle arrived from Earth.

Misty and Kaden almost immediately volunteered to stay behind. They'd wanted to remain on the station as long as possible before any of this happened, and didn't blame Titan for Jala's behavior.

Kirby elected to stay behind, too. After all, without her sister, she didn't feel like she had much of a reason to go home now, and someone had to stay on to take care of the station's systems. She thought her parents would understand.

Ora was the last one to volunteer to wait for the replacement shuttle. She wanted to ensure that NASA started receiving all of their hijacked reports about life on Titan as soon as possible. She felt it was the best way for her to honor Michael, too. She could carry on his work, finishing up the projects he'd been working on before he died.

The conversation then devolved into a debate about whether Jala should be forced to get on the shuttle or not. Those wanting to leave now argued that she couldn't be trusted in such a confined space. Who was to stop her from dismantling the cryosleep chambers and killing all those inside? What if she managed to sabotage the ship's systems somehow?

Those who'd chosen to remain on the station argued that it was worse for her to be on her home turf, able to quietly pick off the remaining inhabitants one by one if she wanted. Due to her years-long reign of terror, and the fact that no one had ever had any idea of what she'd done until now, those staying behind weren't willing to put anything past her.

Even if the Commander remained imprisoned in her room, there was talk of her ability to escape and hunt people down one by one.

Unexpectedly, Commander Shan ended up settling the debate herself when she took the dinner tray Ivy brought to her room, slammed it into the other woman's head, and ran to the hangar.

The others had been so absorbed in deciding what to do with her that it wasn't until the bay door opened that anyone realized something had gone wrong. It all happened so fast; Ivy didn't even get the chance to scream.

Harris was one of the first to arrive at the hangar, but it was locked from the inside, just as it always was when the outer doors opened to the deadly air of Titan.

"Jala's going outside the station!" he shouted, unsure if she'd taken a rover with her or not. They were helpless to do anything until the outer doors closed again. Then they had to go through the time-consuming protocol of cleansing the hangar's air before they could enter.

When it was finally safe to do so, Harris ran into the hangar, frantically calling Jala's name even though he knew she wasn't inside. Instinctively, he knew she wasn't trying to escape. She wanted to be free. Free to enjoy her beautiful, lovely moon on her own terms.

It took twenty minutes for Harris, Kaden, and Ora to suit up and pile into a nearby rover and begin their search. The rest of the group retreated to the safety of the station, and Kirby re-engineered the door so that it would only open from the inside. Harris would comm her when they got back and were ready to come in.

Zevon, meanwhile, had remained at Ivy's side, caring for the gash in her head and going through concussion protocols with her.

"I'm fine, Zevon, I promise," she smiled weakly.

"Nonsense. I'm not leaving your side, Ivy."

☆☆☆☆☆☆☆☆☆

It only took an hour for them to find her. Jala had taken a fairly straightforward path from the station, and they spotted her settled in between two icy outcrops—one of her favorite formations on the moon.

She lovingly called it "Fox Point" because she said the icy spikes looked like rust-colored fox ears. They didn't need to get out of the rover to know she was dead. She'd removed her helmet, arms locked in their final act.

30: After Death…

The survivors held a respectful funeral for Drake the day after Jala took her own way out, and Ora silently wished him well as his body was loaded into the incinerator.

Stria said a quick prayer for him before the somber group took the elevator back to the main level.

✮✮✮✮✮✮✮✮✮

A week later, Harris was organizing everything for the shuttle flight home. *Home, with Stria.* A comforting feeling washed over him, and he blushed crimson.

Half an hour later, the preparations of a lifetime were complete, and he rounded up the survivors, making an unnecessary speech.

Harris ensured that Ivy and Zevon were securely settled into their cryochambers. Before the seals even closed around them, they were already dreaming of opening their own restaurant together and the long happy life ahead of them.

Reid was next, and thankfully, he hopped right in without too much of a fuss.

Stria and Harris had volunteered to remain awake during the long journey home, grateful for every second they could spend with each other.

Kaden, Misty, Kirby, and Ora saw them off, and then began to settle themselves into their new lives on the station. Misty decided to take on the cooking duties, since she had far less cleaning to do with a skeleton crew, and Kaden split his time between helping Kirby with the station's systems, and cooking with Misty. Though he had to admit that spending time with Misty never felt like work at all.

☆☆☆☆☆☆☆☆☆

Ora kept herself busy in the beginning transmitting all the reports that Jala had blocked. The transmissions alone would take her months to complete—after all, she had two years' worth of reports to comm out. Once afraid she'd have nothing worthwhile to do on this station, Ora now felt that nothing could be more fulfilling than announcing to Earth that life had been discovered somewhere else in the Universe.

She was eager to continue the work she'd begun and looked forward to a world of new discoveries stretching out before her over the next few years.

☆☆☆☆☆☆☆☆☆

Kirby was surprised to discover how much she enjoyed life on

Titan without Drake around. She threw herself into her duties with renewed energy, and slowly worked through the grief of losing her sister and Commander Shan, whom she'd always considered a friend. Jala's many, many betrayals bit deep for Kirby, and she was glad to have Misty around. The younger woman knew exactly how she felt, and they shared many tear-filled hours processing their pain together.

All-in-all, Kirby thought they managed pretty well for a four-person crew, and she no longer counted down the years until the final shuttle would arrive.

ABOUT THE AUTHOR

The author lives in the Midwest with her husband and two Catahoula leopard dogs. She's been fascinated with space since she was a little girl, and always wondered what it would be like to walk on the surface of another world. She hopes to be a writer when she grows up.

Printed in Great Britain
by Amazon

20881705R00150